Livin' La Vida Lockdown

BELLE HENDERSON

Dedication

This book is dedicated to Jamie who is my long-suffering Lockdown partner in crime. Special thanks to you and the kids for all your support, patience and inspiration.

Big thanks to my mum, dad, sister and auntie for all your help, guidance and encouragement. I couldn't have done it without you.

Other books by Belle Henderson

Romantic Comedy:
We Can Work it Out

Chapter One

17th March 2020

The tall, navy, shabby windows lookout onto an eerily calm high street. It's exceptionally quiet in the shop today.

I lean on the till, admiring my freshly-painted pastel green nails and look across the road to the quaint little bakery. Gloria, the bakery's owner is staring right back at me, she gives a little wave and then busies herself with cleaning the windowsill. Two elderly customers enjoy a cup of tea and what looks like sausage rolls. My stomach rumbles.

Usually, I'm run off my feet helping people find the perfect outfit for a wedding or posh event. I barely have time to gaze out of the window but as I watch Gloria walk over to her customers, I notice she has quite a bad limp. She told me she sprained it the other day and she's been too busy to take the time off for it to rest and heal. Poor Gloria, she reminds me of The Joker with her white face and dark circles around her eyes, similar hair too. She looks like she could do with a break.

The days always whizz by here but recently it has

slowed to a depressing trickle. To combat the boredom I've tried on everything in the shop now, including the men's stuff. It's becoming a bit of a ghost town in our usually busy seaside town. If I listen intently enough, I can hear the sea, it's trying to speak to me.

Lockdown is looming. The sounds of the wind and sea are suddenly loud. The noise whistles and crashes until it's dancing all around me in a taunting, spiteful whisper. *Lockdown is looming.*

'Alannah, how are you my girl?' The ding of the doorbell and Zeze's husky voice snaps me out of my thoughts and I'm grateful to see her. I really need to stop watching the news and have a break from social media, it's making me feel quite twitchy. Zeze's red, bouncy hair follows in after her as she bounds over to me with open, chubby arms. Her suit is so tight around the arms it's restricting how far she can hold them out.

'Good thanks, Zeze, although a little quiet today but I guess that's to be expected with what's going on.' I hug her, and we exchange two air kisses.

I haven't known Zeze very long. I've been the manager at Emmanuel's for over seven years, Zeze very recently waltzed in and got the job of area manager. A few of the other managers have said she worked for some big designer store in London like Gucci or Burberry before she came here. Surely that's a step down, but it must be less stress, I can imagine the customers being a lot more demanding in London. Coolsbay is only a small seaside town and I know most of my customers personally so they are naturally nicer. My feet are aching much more than usual today despite the shop being completely dead. I've not been feeling myself lately. Tired and out of sorts. I think I need a break as much as Gloria. I look around and realise I haven't done much, and the shop is a bit of a mess. I hope she doesn't notice.

'Ohh, Alannah, you're such a worrier, I can see it written all over your face. This virus is nothing more than what it says it is. A virus. People are worrying over nothing, it's just another type of cold, like a bad case of flu or something.' She pats her hair and rolls her eyes. Her bright pink lipstick covering half her teeth.

'Yeah, I guess you're right, it's just my friend works for the NHS and…'

'No!' Zeze moves closer and shoves her hand up, two inches away from my face. I can smell a mixture of stale tobacco and expensive perfume. It makes me gag and I smile to hide myself flinching.

'Alannah, Alannah. We need to be positive and remain focused. If you think negatively, bad things will happen. That's why this thing is getting out of control. The world is thinking bad thoughts right now and it's breeding this thing, this fear, this pretend virus. Now let's see what you've done with the new stock.' She smiles a bright smile with her pink-lipstick teeth. As I take her over to the display, I decide not to tell her about her teeth today. It's not a pretend virus, many people have actually died. It's not just a common cold or the flu. I remind myself of the main symptoms again, persistent cough, high temperature and loss of taste and smell. I've certainly not been enjoying my food as much lately. Could it be I'm losing my sense of taste? Could I have it?

A customer enters the shop and we both desperately say hello and ask if she needs help, probably a little too enthusiastically. I watch as Zeze pushes it one step further and takes it upon herself to follow the poor woman around asking about her day and how she can help in various ways.

The customer frowns. 'I just want to browse, okay?' she says with a raised voice. My toes curl.

'Yes, of course.' Zeze flashes her pink teeth in a big startled grin and I struggle to stifle a giggle.

Zeze goes back to appraising my mannequins and starts changing everything, then changing it all back again. She unties a purple sash from the mannequin's waist and ties it around its neck. She shakes her head quickly then swiftly unties it and puts it around the waist again, fussing over the size of the bow for way too long.

This is the usual protocol.

I wonder what else she does as an area manager apart from fuss with the mannequins and check what our best sellers are. Maybe I could be an area manager. Get paid more and do much less, sounds ideal. My mind starts to wander again as I watch her ruin a mannequin outfit completely by swapping a beautiful box cream jacket for a long brown one.

Gucci, my arse.

'Okay, Alannah, I think we need to pretty it up a bit in here. I'm sorry to say the shop is looking a little untidy. As it's quiet, shall we give it a little clean and spruce?' Her eyes bore into mine, blinking, big long steady blinks. Of course, the answer is yes.

My head nods and I automatically follow after Zeze to get the cleaning products and vacuum.

'It's really hot in here don't you think'? I hear myself say to Zeze. 'Shall I turn the heating off?'

'Alannah, it's four degrees outside.' She stops ferreting around in the cleaning box and looks me up and down. 'Are you alright?' she asks.

I nod with a small smile and switch on the hoover.

Beads of sweat start to roll down my forehead. It really is hot in here. It can't be four degrees, twenty-four more like.

It's going to happen, we don't know when, but it's inevitable. People are already starting to self-isolate and you can almost taste the fear. I'd be lying if I said I didn't feel a little unsettled. I've seen it on the news which I'm following like an obsessed tabloid freak, checking my phone fifteen times a day for an update to see if it's the UK's turn yet. Many countries in Europe are now on complete lockdown, everything is closed, non-essential shops, restaurants, pubs, schools, you name it. People aren't allowed out apart from shopping for essentials and thirty minutes to an hour of daily exercise. Soon, it will be us and then what will happen to my job? To Jake's job? How will my family and friends cope? I think of my friend Laura, she's a Paramedic Practitioner at the local doctors' surgery, she hasn't seen her family or friends for three weeks already for fear of making her loved ones ill.

I suddenly feel quite queasy and hot.

Urgh, I feel incredibly hot now. I stop to have a little rest and take my thin crochet cardigan off. As expected, it makes no difference at all.

I'm still super-hot.

Too hot.

The smells coming from the cleaning products are making me feel lightheaded. I look at Zeze and she's going hell for leather on the till. She's taken her jacket off and her chubby little arms are violently flapping under her cream blouse. There must be a lot of germs on that till. I think of Louise, our Saturday girl, who doesn't appear to like washing too much. I make a mental note to have a gentle word with her.

My mouth is now full of saliva.

Nausea overcomes me.

Urgh.

I need to get out of here.

I'm going to be sick.

♥ ♥ ♥

'Alannah, Alannah, wake up. Wake up!' Everything is dark at first. I open my eyes to a bird's eye view of Zeze's nostrils as she slaps me around the face with something cold. Is that her hand? A wet fish? No, I think it's the dish cloth and it has my mopped-up bean juice on it from lunch. My head is pounding. The stench of bin beans, tobacco and strong perfume hits me. I definitely haven't lost my sense of smell. I turn away from Zeze to try to find somewhere else to aim other than her, I'm too weak to get up.

Oh God. There's vomit all over her Ted Baker suit, her knees covered in orange. Was that me? It appears I was too late. This is too embarrassing; I want to hide away from the world. Another big acidic heave leaves me decorating her black, shiny Dior shoes with burnt orange blobby sick. Maybe a lockdown wouldn't be such a bad thing for me. Definitely not living my best life right now.

I'm sitting out the back of the shop in the tiny staff room, next to the old, dirty microwave. Zeze has been quite kind, looking after me and I feel like a complete bitch for not telling her about the lipstick on her teeth, perhaps I over reacted. She's reassured me not to worry and knows I'm not myself today. Thank God I am usually good at my job or this could be a downward spiral for me and my career in retail. This store is always in the top five out of the forty *Emmanuel* stores in the UK. I've also had many complimentary emails sent to Head Office from satisfied customers so I am safe in the knowledge that I am generally rather excellent at my job. Zeze disappears to scout the shop floor for customers only to return minutes later. She shrugs her shoulders.

'Jake is on his way, Alannah. I found his number on your next of kin sheet. He'll be here any minute. I thought it best that someone come and get you, I'm not sure you're well enough to drive. I'll cash up and lock up, it's almost closing time anyway.' Frantically, she wipes down her suit and shoes again with a clean wet cloth. Her chubby little hands working extra hard to make sure all signs of my vomit have gone.

'Thank you, Zeze, I'm so sorry,' I mumble, because that's all I can manage, I just want to go home. I walked in today anyway, but a lift home *is* needed right now.

'Babe, what the hell? Hi, Zeze.' Jake appears from behind the curtain separating the tiny kitchen and the seating area. It's a small shop but the company certainly did scrimp on the tiny cell like, staff room. Jake has his sports gear on, he must have had a client as this is usually his day off from the gym.

He looks fit. I stink of sick.

'Hi, I'm fine now,' I say as he comes closer to inspect me. 'I just had a funny turn, I think.'

He smirks and rubs his bare arms then walks over and puts an arm around my shoulder. He smiles at Zeze. She licks her lips slowly and flashes her teeth at him. I think she winks at him too, but it could be an eyelash stuck in her eye.

'Hi, Jake. Excuse me, duty calls, I'll be back in a moment.' Zeze simpers, before marching off to the back of the staff room. We both watch her bounce off. I'm glad she's gone.

'Babe, is this the side effects of last night?' He laughs his braying donkey laugh. It instantly cheers me up.

'What, no! And don't say stuff like that in front of Zeze,' I whisper, pulling his arm closer.

'She's can't hear, she's in the bog.' He laughs again into my ear.

'No, it's not the side effects from last night, I only had two glasses of wine,' I mumble. I possibly had more but no way would it have this effect on me and especially not this late in the afternoon. 'It was just a funny turn, people have them,' I say with a sigh whilst making a mental note to google all symptoms of the virus again and why people have funny turns.

'Okay, Funny Turn, let's get you home.'

Chapter Two

This last week has gone by in a slow, boring blur apart from the somewhat awkward conversation with Louise about her body odour.

Apparently, she doesn't believe in using soap and is letting science do its thing. I told her the science clearly isn't working so please could she wash as some of the customers and other members of staff have complained. I didn't tell her that the assistant manager caught her rinsing out her menstrual cup in the kitchen sink. Just gross. Louise told me that's discrimination for people who want to use their natural probiotics and she will be phoning HR to complain. She says that Willow in HR will understand as she is also an anti-washer. It appears there's now a whole pro-stinky armpits community. Great.

After the embarrassing events of last week with Zeze, I googled the symptoms of the virus and I was relived for all of five minutes that sickness and passing out are not side effects. Phew. It then dawned on me that I just might be pregnant. After trying to mentally calculate my last period, I still couldn't work it out which (unbeknown to Jake) led me to buy a test. The test came back negative and rather than feeling relieved, I feel disappointed. I've always wanted children and Jake knows that, perhaps it's time to broach the subject again and see what he says. Last time it was a maybe so perhaps this time it will be a yes. We've been together long enough and whilst marriage is important to me, it can wait. At thirty-one, my ovaries are ready and waiting. I'd always imagined my children walking down the aisle with me and being part of the big day anyway, their chubby little faces watching Mummy and Daddy get married. What could be cuter?

'Babe, Bojo is on in five minutes,' Jake calls from the living room as I pad down the stairs, freshly-washed hair up in a towel, fluffy white dressing gown and mud mask on. It's pamper night this evening. Jake says he likes to be well maintained so he often joins me in my beauty regimes. It's quite endearing really.

'Hey, when can I take this thing off then? It's itching my face already.' Jake frowns and touches his face, poking and then rubbing his fingers together, examining the brown, clay-like sludge.

'It's just drying, that's all. Thirty minutes for a deep cleanse, after the speech should be fine. Stop touching,' I say, slapping his hand away and then grinning at him, before sitting down on the sofa.

'Right. Let's see what Boris has to say.' I rub my hands on my knees.

'Come on, Bojo!' Jake shouts, punching the air.

'Jake, this isn't a boxing match, it's people's lives.'

'It's boxing *fight* babe, not match,' he corrects.

I roll my eyes and turn up the volume on the TV. Bojo begins to speak.

'Good Evening,
The coronavirus is the biggest threat this country has faced for decades – and this country is not alone.
All over the world we are seeing the devastating impact of this invisible killer.
And so tonight I want to update you on the latest steps we are taking to fight the disease and what you can do to help.'

'Bojo looks knackered,' Jake comments, turning up the TV.

'He always looks like that; he's got a baby on the way too,' I reply, scoffing down a packet of Maltesers. Boris goes on to say how the NHS won't be able to handle it, if it gets out of hand. There simply won't be enough beds, doctors or nurses. Jake and I exchange wide-eyed glances. This is real. More people will die and not just from the virus.

'So it's vital to slow the spread of the disease.
Because that is the way we reduce the number of people needing hospital treatment at any one time, so we can protect the NHS's ability to cope - and save more lives.
And that's why we have been asking people to stay at home during this pandemic.'

I suddenly feel guilty and very stupid for going out last night. It was just a few drinks in our local pub with my brother but still, there could have been people in there who had it. I guess Zeze wasn't the only one not taking this seriously, it was me too.

'From this evening I must give the British people a very simple instruction – you must stay at home. Because the critical thing we must do is stop the disease spreading between households.

That is why people will only be allowed to leave their home for the following very limited purposes:

shopping for basic necessities, as infrequently as possible;

one form of exercise a day – for example a run, walk, or cycle – alone or with members of your household;

any medical need, to provide care or to help a vulnerable person;

and travelling to and from work, but only where this is absolutely necessary and cannot be done from home.

That's all – these are the only reasons you should leave your home.

You should not be meeting friends. If your friends ask you to meet, you should say no.

You should not be meeting family members who do not live in your home.'

Boris continues to say how we should only be going out shopping for essentials. If we don't follow the rules, we could be fined or worse. He states he will be closing all shops that sell non-essential goods including clothing, electronic stores and other premises including libraries, playgrounds and outdoor gyms, and places of worship. So that's *Emmanuel's* closing then. No social gatherings at all, no weddings, baptisms or any other ceremony apart from funerals. They are stopping everything. You must only see the people you live with. That's it, only parks will remain open for exercise. We're going to be imprisoned in our own homes for most of the day.

'No Prime Minister wants to enact measures like this.

I know the damage that this disruption is doing and will do to people's lives, to their businesses and to their jobs.'

'What are they going to do about your pay then? Will you still get paid? Jake asks. His face is bone dry now and the mask is starting to flake.

'I don't know, he just said something about support for businesses, whatever that will be, I don't know,' I reply, touching my face as Bojo says they will review in three weeks. Hopefully it will have improved by then and we can start to return to some sort of normality. If we miss out on money, it hopefully won't be very much.

'I want to thank everyone who is working flat out to beat the virus.
Everyone from the supermarket staff to the transport workers to the carers to the nurses and doctors on the frontline.
But in this fight we can be in no doubt that each and every one of us is directly enlisted.
Each and every one of us is now obliged to join together.
To halt the spread of this disease.
To protect our NHS and to save many, many thousands of lives and I know that as they have in the past so many times, the people of this country will rise to that challenge.
And we will come through it stronger than ever.
We will beat the coronavirus and we will beat it together.
And therefore, I urge you at this moment of national emergency to stay at home, protect our NHS and save lives. Thank you.'

Jake switches off the TV and bites his lip as he stares into my face. Perhaps his expression is enhanced by the cracking and flaking facemask but it's the first time I've seen him look worried about it. It's the first time it feels real for him. His blue eyes look like sad, empty swimming pools.

'This is absolutely mental, what the hell?' he exclaims.

'It's awful but for the best. We don't want to catch it, or anyone we know for that matter,' I reply. My thoughts turn to my brother Beau, he has asthma and this thing attacks the lungs. When he was five, he suffered an awful attack and ended up in intensive care for a week. I remember it vividly, my mum was distraught, we all were. The asthma isn't so bad now, but he still has it, not helped by smoking recreational drugs most nights, but Beau does what Beau wants.

'I guess we can kiss goodbye to our holiday too,' Jake says rubbing his forehead. My dreams of soaking up the sun in Sardinia quickly turn to images of rain and boredom.

'Maybe, but it's not until May, it might be over by then,' I offer. Surely it will be over by then. They're reviewing in three weeks.

'Yeah, hopefully. Probably.' Jake shrugs, looks at his phone and laughs to himself. 'Babe, look at what Flynn just sent me.'

I lean over from my side of the sofa to see a meme of Boris with the words *you can only go for one walk a day* plastered across his forehead. Underneath is a photo of The Proclaimers, with *say no more* written beneath them. Boris didn't actually say how long we could go outside for, just that we can go out once a day, it's typical of Flynn to notice and make a joke. I've no doubt there will still be exercise freaks out all day walking and running, although maybe not quite for five hundred miles like The Proclaimers suggest. Flynn is Jake's best mate and they were practically stuck at the hip when we first met. It took Flynn a little while to warm to me as I had stolen his wingman, which was understandable. We get on great now though and that's just as well as he lives across the road, in the flat opposite us.

'Flynn said we will have to do a social distancing games night with him and Becky on the balconies, instead of them coming over,' Jake continues, sounding slightly more upbeat.

'Yeah, at least we have the balconies to chat to friends and the beach for walks, it could be a lot worse.' Beau also lives in the flats, adjacent to Flynn, but that's mainly so I can keep an eye on him.

'I know, babe, it'll be fine. Anyway, I think the gyms will still be open won't they, it's essential, keeping fit.' He sniffs and tosses his head to the side to get his hair out of his eyes but a bit stays stuck to his face, embedded in the long overdue facemask.

'Hmmm, yeah, I guess, but people can do that outside,' I mutter. 'I think they may have to close.'

'Dunno, I guess I'll just have to wait to hear from the big man.' He shrugs his shoulders.

'And I don't think you can do personal training for the time being as it isn't family or someone you live with,' I continue.

'What, no way?' he says, sucking in his bottom lip, like a sulky teenager. I wonder if he was even listening to his beloved Bojo.

'It's okay, we have some savings if anything happens,' I reassure. We're very lucky that we do because I'm not certain we will get paid if we aren't in work. Maybe now isn't the right time to broach the subject of trying for a baby. 'Jake, if we are stuck in together with no work then we will just have to make the most of all this time together and come up with our own entertainment. We can do date nights, binge watch as much Netflix as we like and there might be the odd massage night,' I say winking. Yes, we can slow right down for a little while and use this time to recharge and reignite our relationship. It could be a lot worse for us.

'Oh, babe now you're talking, why don't we practice these other ways of entertainment right now!' He whips off his t-shirt for a massage or maybe he has something else in mind. He leans over and kisses my neck. This is going to be bliss in a way, just me and him in our own little cocoon, concentrating totally on us. I'm enjoying the neck kisses, despite our crusty faces, when I notice a notification pop up on my phone.

Zeze has just sent an email to all managers. That was quick. We are not to come in tomorrow and must inform all staff that there will be no work until further notice.

'Yeah, good idea Jake,' I say over his shoulder, distracted.

There will be a Zoom call with all managers at 9am to discuss the plan of action and further details.

Oh shit.

Chapter Three

The next day

My laptop is opened for the first time in months.

Dust and mug marks show it in a very sorry state. Phones do everything don't they, so I haven't bothered using it for quite a while. I switch it on and the whirring circle monotonously turns round until it eventually decides to comply and let me in. Seven managers will be included in the Zoom call for the South West of England, including me and I don't want to be last. I've allowed plenty of time for this painfully slow process which I imagine is how the Zoom call will go too, painful, slow and depressing. The invitation pops up in front of me and I hover my mouse over it before hitting the button. Click.

'Hi guys.' Zeze pops up. It's just Zeze and I in the call so far. I wish I'd waited a bit longer but that's me, always early no matter how hard I try. Sometimes it's a curse, not a blessing.

'Hey, Zeze.' I wave and see my face staring back at me. I'm so glad that I washed my hair last night. The thing about Zoom calls is that you still have to make an effort, at least from the waist up anyway.

'Alannah, how are you feeling now?' she asks, moving her big hair behind her ears and leaning forward to study me. Straight into it. We haven't spoken since that humiliating day and I was hoping she would just leave it. My thoughts turn to the recent 111 call I had with a nurse who (after many personal questions) told me it sounded like I'd probably reacted that way due to anxiety and stress about the virus. She said it was very common at the moment and told me to call them if it happens again. It's astonishing how an emotion like fear can have that much of an effect on your body, making you physically sick.

'Yes. All good now, thanks. It must have been something I'd eaten.' I grimace at the thought of the beans on her suit and shoes and hope she doesn't notice me turning the same shade as my sick on camera. I did send her some flowers to apologise and say thank you for looking after me. She obviously didn't realise that this was also a keep quiet bribe. Please someone else enter the call.

Someone.

Anyone.

'You should go and get it checked out, Alannah, at your doctors. I'm sure you've heard it all before but you are extremely thin, it's not healthy…' Zeze begins. I can feel a long lecture coming on and I zone out as the smell memory of tobacco and strong perfume dance around mockingly in my nostrils. I push air out of them to try and get rid of the smell, making a loud snorting sound that causes Zeze to frown and stop talking for a second. I say nothing so she carries on her lecture, whilst I stare into space, not listening.

It makes me laugh how people deem it totally acceptable to call people extremely thin but it's definitely not okay to call someone extremely fat. Maybe I should try calling someone fat one day to show my concern, just as a social experiment. Or maybe not, no doubt I'd be slapped across the face. Slim is the term I prefer; I've always been slim and probably always will be. It's in my genetic makeup. Our entire family are built like tall stick insects, the men are even thinner. My brother Beau is a towering six feet five inches tall and weighs about twelve stone even though he eats around six thousand calories a day, five thousand of that is chocolate and crisps. What I would give to swap my pancake bum for a bubble butt like Flynn's girlfriend, Becky, however no number of squats would create that for me. It would be like trying to make a big cookie dough muffin from a thin little biscuit base. Impossible.

'Hello, hello, can anyone hear me?' Clara enters the call and saves me from any further conversation about my sicky episode. Then Nicola's face pops up, quickly followed by Lisa, Daniel and Cherry. Everyone says their polite hellos and waits in anticipation.

'Okay, guys, I think we're just waiting for Lance so let's just give it a minute and talk amongst ourselves,' Zeze announces. Nicola and Clara start talking about their kids and Cherry asks Zeze where she got her fabulous top from. The usual arse licking from her. Daniel is staring at the screen, with his fluffy, grey cat on his lap. It has big green eyes and looks very expensive. He's talked about this cat before at managers' meetings, I think he told me his name is Dave or some other name belonging to a human. My phone lights up and I glance down to see a message on WhatsApp from Lisa.

Lisa: *Nice hair gorgeous, loving the blonde bob but also how hunky does Daniel look? I'm gonna be drooling over him like an old hungry dog during this call.*

I smirk and start typing my reply. Daniel, unaware of the pervert that is Lisa, is trying to be attentive to his grumpy looking cat, who keeps batting him off like a pesky fly.

Me: *Haha. Stop. You dirty old dog.*

Lisa is forty-five and happily married but that doesn't stop her from noticing an aesthetically pleasing person and pointing it out. Her husband doesn't seem to mind (or so she says). I watch her husband in the background ushering the kids out of the room, one of them starts throwing a tantrum and refuses to leave. Lisa doesn't flinch or turn around and instead, she looks down, smiling at her phone.

Lisa: *I see Daniel likes stroking pussy. Hahahahaha.*
Me: *Yuck. You are something else, Lisa.*

I swallow my hysterics, compose myself and stare back at the screen blankly. With my best poker face on, I avoid all eye contact with Lisa who is now grinning from ear to ear in my peripheral vision. This is a serious call. I must not laugh at Lisa. Zeze coughs, then clears her throat to speak.

'Okay, I'm not sure what's happened with Lance but we're just going to have to get started without him and I'll bring him up to speed later.' Everyone nods along and waits for the much anticipated and ominous news.

'I take it everyone watched the update from Boris Johnson last night? she adds. Everyone says yes and nods along again. Waiting. She continues.

'Okay, good. So just to bring you all up to speed we had a crisis call last night with Manni that lasted two hours. He's decided that all *Emmanuel's* stores are now closed until further notice. Selling luxury wedding and events wear means we are not essential workers. I think we can all agree no one will be going to events like these for a little while so our services are not required. All managers will get paid their full wage for this month as normal however we will have to go on skeleton staff from now on and make a few cuts. We will then need to review pay for next month for managers. This will be done in a couple of weeks when we know where we are with everything.' She gulps in a big breath of air then pauses. Gasps echo around the call. Clara looks as if she's about to cry. Nicola starts violently coughing. We wait until she's finished as nothing would be heard over that hacking cough. Does she have the virus? Has she passed it on to all her staff?

'Does anyone have any questions so far?' Zeze asks, blinking. Cherry pipes up and I imagine everyone inwardly groaning.

'Sorry, Zeze, a few questions. Are you going to tell us who we need to make redundant? Will you be advising them or is it down to us? Are our jobs safe as managers? Do we know how long this will last?' When can we start to employ more staff again?' Woah, slow down Cherry. There's definitely a reason why Lisa calls her *the machine gun*. She's one of those people where her name doesn't match her personality or face. To me, Cherry sounds like a sweet, soft name. This Cherry is the complete opposite with a hard, angular looking face and an aggressive, snappy manner. Zeze blows air out of her mouth and then speaks slowly in a low voice.

'It will be down to you as managers to tell the staff and Head Office will follow up with the paper work. All staff on zero-hour contracts will have to be let go with immediate effect. We need to protect the business. Are your jobs safe? For the time being yes, but…'

'So that's basically everyone gone then apart from us and the assistant managers?' Daniel interrupts. His dulcet Manchester tones make him sound calm and collected.

'Yes, that's right Daniel, we need to protect our business. This thing isn't going to go away overnight,' Zeze clips back at him. That's not what she said to me on her last visit to the shop, she said everyone was overreacting. I wonder if she told Manni that she thought it was just a little cold. She's certainly changed her tune.

'But people will lose their jobs overnight. Right, wow. That's brutal,' he replies still calm, as he busies himself getting his cat down off his shoulders and onto his lap again. I notice a guitar in the background and remember him telling me at a mangers' meeting once that he also sings. I try to imagine what his singing voice would sound like whilst Zeze lectures him.

'Yes. They will. It's an extremely unusual time and if we don't act quickly then the business will not survive. It is *brutal* as you call it but necessary. At least this way they'll be able to claim job seeker's allowance, or get another job instead of waiting around hoping it'll soon be over. The supermarkets have vacancies, apparently,' Zeze explains firmly, with conviction. She has been well trained for this meeting it seems. Well at least smelly Louise's complaint won't get far with HR now. Ha! Small blessings and all that but she doesn't deserve this, no one does. Lisa starts to speak but then her screen freezes and she is locked in limbo with her mouth wide open, catching flies. If I wasn't so stressed, I'd find that hilarious.

'Zeze, do you want us to phone the staff on video call or can we do it on the normal phone,' Clara asks and I feel embarrassed for her, what is normal phone? She is very nice but common sense is not her friend. A little extra dark square appears on the screen. It must be Lance; we've already been on the call almost fifteen minutes.

'I think do whatever you are comfortable with, Clara. If you think they will get upset then they probably don't want you to see their facial expressions but it's your call, you know your staff better than me.' Zeze shrugs her shoulders which makes her big bosoms bounce. She then does a little mock sad face to show how the staff might look whilst being told they don't have a job anymore, pointing to her downturned mouth with a long pink finger nail.

Clara smiles sweetly, still looking tearful. The dark square who we assume is Lance, and not some hacker, starts to lighten enough for everyone to see movement. My phone pings. It's Lisa. Her face on the screen still frozen in time with her mouth wide open.

Lisa: *What is Lance doing?*
Lisa: *Oh my god. Aghhhhhhhhhhh!!!*

It's a hairy arse on screen. It appears to belong to Lance. He slowly turns around, giving everyone a full show of something even hairier. Nicola grimaces and waves at the screen in the hope of getting his attention and making it stop. Clara hasn't appeared to notice yet and still looks like she's going to cry or maybe she *has* noticed and still wants to cry. Daniel pushes his cat off his lap and lets out a big guffaw in his chair, flinging his arms back and bashing his guitar off the wall with a big clunk in the process. Cherry has her hand over her mouth, the first time I've seen her speechless. Ever.

Zeze is shouting. Hysterical, sounding almost excited.

'Lance, Lance, can you hear us? Turn on your screen. I repeat, turn on your screen now.'

'We can see him, Zeze, that's not the problem,' Daniel says, dryly.

'Put some pants on, Lance! There's some on the chair behind you!' I shriek, in the hope that he might somehow hear me. Daniel and Nicola start laughing, and my hand flings up to my mouth to try and stuff the words back in. What a prat.

'I don't think he has his mic on,' Cherry whispers in shock.

'I don't think he knows it's on at all,' Nicola adds as she looks away smirking.

'My eyes, my eyes!' Lisa's face unfreezes and she is now in full blown crying laughter. This is too much.

Lance is full frontal, appearing to perform a series of lunges, with everything swinging. He stands up again then bends down to touch his toes. We get a glimpse of his face as he bends down, completely peaceful and at one with the stretch. Pure innocent, naked yoga joy.

'Oh my God. I've messaged him but he hasn't seen it. I'll try again,' Daniel says. He picks up his phone and starts typing. His frown doesn't hide the crinkly eyes and big grin as his shoulders bob up and down in silence.

'I've messaged him too,' I say with my head in my hands, peeking through my fingers. The poor guy is never going to live this down. This is cringingly uncomfortable.

'I'm ringing him now,' Zeze announces. She is absolutely manic and her hair looks twice the size it normally does from her pulling at it constantly.

'So am I,' adds Cherry the arse lick, looking fuming on behalf of Zeze. Her small mouth, looking even smaller than usual, as if that's even possible, resembles a cat's bum hole.

Lance pulses a few more times to try and get a further stretch past his toes (which is actually very impressive) then stands up and reaches his arms up to the ceiling, revealing all his glory yet again. Woah, that is one hairy man. I imagine he does these stretches all the time to set himself up for the day ahead. Little does he know that soon these stretches will be tainted. He probably won't ever want to do them again once he finds out about his secret audience.

'Seriously, shall we just end the call? Lance wouldn't want us to see this,' cries Clara. It's all too much for her and she's gone, tapped out.

'Wait. Someone is coming into the room. Is that his girlfriend?' Lisa asks, leaning forward for a closer look. 'She's giving him his phone! She's giving him his phone!' she screeches in excitement, clapping her hands together.

Everyone holds their breath.

Lance. Still naked. Casually he takes the phone from his girlfriend and gives her bum a big smack that echoes around the call before scrolling through to check his messages. It takes a few seconds for the penny to drop. He throws a quick panicked glance at the laptop. His head then bobs around, desperately scouting and searching the room for a solution as he remains rooted to the spot. He picks up what looks like an old pizza box off his chest of drawers, and covers his bits, back and front. He attempts to sprint out of the room as his girlfriend looks on confused. His foot is just out of the door when a slice of half-eaten pizza slides down the back of his leg. He pauses for a split second, dying inside I expect, as the pizza plops onto the floor. A sign of all his dignity leaving him. Forever.

The computer screen goes blank. The call has been ended.

My phone lights up.

Daniel: *You were so funny shouting at Lance to put his pants on. I almost died laughing. I'm gonna ring Lance now, he'll be alright after I've taken the piss out of him for a good hour for doing naked exercise and shitting out a slice of pizza.'*

Me: *Haha thanks, Daniel. I can't believe I said that! Let me know how he is. I can't believe he didn't know he had logged in to the call.*

Daniel: *Stranger things have happened. He's made of tough stuff. He'll probably find it funny after he's gotten over the shock.*

Zeze sends through an email at lunch time detailing the discussion and answering any questions we had in the meeting that weren't answered then. There is no mention of Lance, the big elephant in the room. She ended the call but I can't help thinking she should have ended it a lot earlier and we shouldn't have kept watching Lance's hairy, naked appendages. Zeze signs off by saying that all communication will be done on email from now on and we must await further updates.

Chapter Four

Easter Monday – Three weeks since lockdown

'Hey, babe, what are we watching today then? Fancy this new series on Netflix?' Jake's sitting in his grey jogging bottoms and his white, now turning grey, t-shirt. He scrolls down to another mundane celebrity dating show. I can't stomach any more TV; we've spent the whole of Easter weekend slumped on the sofa and it's starting to wear a bit thin.

'Naah. Let's go to the beach, I need a walk.'

'Ahh, babe, but we haven't completed Netflix yet and I'm hungry again,' he moans, patting his much softer than usual midriff. Jake is certainly adjusting well to his new lockdown life as a giant couch potato.

'Jake, Netflix is not a game; we don't have to complete it. Come on, get off your arse.'

Jake throws his head back like a moody teen and groans like Chewbacca before reluctantly peeling himself up off the sofa. He brushes crisp and biscuit crumbs off his lap onto my newly vacuumed floor. I bite my tongue and let it go. Again. He bit my head off the last time I said something.

'Come on, this will do us good, bit of sea air and

exercise,' I say to encourage him to hurry up as he slowly searches for his trainers.

We step outside and it's a gorgeous sunny day. I've got a new dress on. The late-night internet spending struggle is real right now and I really shouldn't be doing it, especially as I'm now furloughed. Yes furloughed. Wouldn't it be great to get paid 80 percent of your salary forever and never have to go back? It's going to be so hard to go back to work, I don't miss it at all.

The few people on the beach and my new best buds at the supermarket will give zero shits how I look in my new dress, but it cheers me up no end to be dressed in something nice. I feel all cute and feminine in my new floaty yellow summer dress, white flip flops and straw hat. We wander the short fifteen-minute walk down to the beach and let the cobwebs blow away on the journey. It would be good to own a dog right now, at least it would be an excuse to get out more.

I'm really surprised we haven't been outside more considering Jake's a fitness instructor but he says he's having a bit of a rest before he records his fitness videos. He was working six days a week, sometimes seven so he does deserve it and what better time to do it than now, but I can't help thinking he may have missed the boat. Flynn is posting every day with his workouts; we sometimes watch from the balcony as that's where he films himself. He's also making money from sponsors who want him to wear their sports clothes, it appears our Flynn has quite the online following. He's soaring whilst Jake is slobbing.

We approach the top of the hill and admire the sea glistening in the distance, inviting us down into its glorious sparkling loveliness. We're so lucky to have this. *This* is my garden.

'Oi oi,' a voice calls from somewhere on the beach. I squint to see who it is but I'm distracted by a stunning blue bird, one I've never seen before. Everything is so much brighter and more beautiful than I remember. The smooth white sand and clear blue sea remind me of a pretty seaside postcard. Amazingly, there isn't an empty beer can to be seen. Pure, beautiful bliss, and I live here.

'Babe. It's Beau.' Jake points at my brother who's waving at us from the beach.

Joint in hand, Beau comes jogging over in giant leaps with no shoes on.

'Beau, stay back,' I boom, holding my hand out, feeling like a police officer. 'Two metres remember.'

'Oh yeah, sorry sis. You're the first humans I've seen in weeks so I got a bit excited.' He laughs and finger combs his long straggly hair away from his face, revealing his slightly bloodshot eyes.

'What are you on about? We see you almost every day on the balconies.' I narrow my eyes at him, is he really that high?

'This is my last one today,' Beau says ignoring me and looking longingly at his massive joint. 'My dealer's been busted. Batshit Steve said not to contact the other local dealers as the police are really cracking down on it so it's not worth the risk. Plus, I don't have a car so…'

'Yeah, we'll see how long that lasts,' Jake mumbles, rolls his eyes and turns his back on us to watch some people jogging along the sea front.

'It's probably a good thing, Beau.' I smile sympathetically. 'You really should quit.'

'I know, sis, I'm okay with it, I think. I've been meditating and doing yoga. Trying to give my mind a real chill out and get back to basics, man.'

'That spliff is gonna give your mind a real chill out, mate.' Jake snorts with his back still turned and his shoulders hunched up.

'Woah, alright, Johnny Bravo. Jeez what's up with muscles?' Beau laughs a high-pitched laugh then starts doing muscle man poses behind Jake's back with the joint still in his mouth. His long, lanky arms make him look like a giant, emaciated ape.

'You heard from Mum today?' I ask, changing the subject as Jake wanders off towards the sea. He has been super grumpy lately. I don't know what's got into him.

'She's alright, she's got Gary, hasn't she,' Beau answers then gets into character by putting his hands on his hips and speaking in Mum's posh phone voice. 'But at least I'm not going to be upset missing any grandkids like all my friends do because I don't have any to miss, do I? Honestly, I thought I would have at least one by now, Beau, my darling boy.' Beau reverts back to his usual stance and laughs at his own impression of Mum. My brother, ever the comedian.

'Oh God, you need to hurry up and give her some then,' I tease.

'Yeah man, my kids will be the best little shits ever. Anyway, it's not me she's expecting them from, is it?' He raises an eyebrow and flicks his ash onto the sand while blowing smoke out of the side of his mouth.

'Well I guess it would help if you got a girlfriend first.' I raise an eyebrow back.

'I don't need a girlfriend for that, it's 2020. But come to think of it, your mate Laura is quite fit. She'd make good looking, intelligent offspring.'

'She is a catch but a little bit busy saving lives at the moment,' I state, whilst making a mental note to give her a call soon.

'Oh yeah, how's that going?'

'Not good, the surgery doesn't have enough PPE and it's making the staff more stressed than they need to be. They have enough to worry about, caring for desperately ill people let alone risk catching it themselves. Some staff have even had to wear binbags to work. It's awful,' I explain, feeling annoyed for Laura.

'Diabolical. It makes me so sad, man. We should raise some money like that Captain Tom Moore dude, I might do some laps of my garden.' Beau blows out big O shaped smoke rings before dropping his joint onto the sand.

'One, you don't have a garden and two, you're not an adorable pensioner who served in the war and won many medals. It won't sell.' I pick the offensive butt off the sand and give it back to him. He stuffs it into his jeans' pocket, not phased.

'True. Why don't you make them some masks then?' Beau suggests.

'Really?' I answer as I watch Jake start to march back over with a face like thunder.

'Yeah, you can sew, help them out man, spread the love,' he says with his arms out wide. I used to sew before I met Jake. Before life got busy. It might not be a bad idea.

'I don't have a sewing machine; it would take ages by hand.'

'Borrow Mum's.'

'No harm in asking, I guess. Mum could just leave it outside her house for me to collect.'

'Exactly that. You could also hit me up some green, there's some dude I know around the corner from

Mum's.'

'Absolutely no way. You're giving up anyway,' I squawk then go to lunge forward to push him, before remembering I can't do that anymore. Beau jumps out of the way and laughs.

'I know, just joking, sis.' He sniffs and looks down at his bare feet, when he wiggles his long toes in the sand his feet look like two bendy rakes.

'Hey, you ready to go now, babe?' Jake asks as he appears by my side, looking as grumpy as he did before, if not more.

'What? Home? We haven't even done a walk yet?' I moan, sounding like the typical whiney girlfriend.

'By the time we get home it will be nearly an hour so that's our time up.'

I'd forgotten we're only allowed out for an hour a day. I glance at my watch, we've been out thirty minutes in total, we could walk for another fifteen but it's not worth the argument. For a peaceful life I relent and nod.

'See ya later, guys,' Beau calls out as we part ways. 'Hey, we should get a takeaway one night and all have it together on the balconies, get Flynn and Becky involved too.'

'Sounds good,' I shout back. 'See you soon!'

We walk back to the flat in silence. I'm annoyed we're going back now, my only chance out of the house all day. Really should have just stayed and told Jake to head back without me. We get in and Jake slopes off to play his new computer game. His new lockdown hobby is gaming. Before now I hadn't seen him play one computer game but everyone has their coping mechanisms, I guess. Drinking and eating appear to be mine, I've easily doubled the amount I used to drink.

Lisa said she's put on half a stone since lockdown and she' s aiming to get cut out of her house and air lifted out by a crane by the end of it. Daniel's been writing songs and hanging out with his cat, he's working on a funny little ditty about lockdown apparently.

'Just off out to give Betty her supplies, be back in a bit,' I call out to Jake. He grunts back. Betty, my elderly next-door neighbour, is high risk so is self-isolating for twelve weeks, I've offered to do her shopping for her until she's able to go out again. I walk the couple of steps to her door and give it a few knocks before setting down her supplies, being careful to step back and allow enough space between us.

'Hello, love.' Betty answers the door smiling. Her tiny frame drowning in a floor length floral skirt and yellow t-shirt. She looks so frail.

'Hi, Bet, how's it going today? Just dropping off your bits. Sorry they didn't have any eggs.' I point to the flowery shopping bags she gave me.

'Don't worry, love, I was just going to make a cake for something to do anyway, it's not desperate.' She smiles again, folding her arms across her tiny body. We chat for a while about her ailments and her deceased husband, before she fills me in on her kids and grandkids and what they're all up to. She has three children and two of them live in Australia. I end up telling Bet all about my plans to help with PPE and she is extremely encouraging. Bet used to be a seamstress so she said she would help me with instructions if I get stuck with the sewing machine.

'Oh hello.' She grins. Stopping mid conversation, she waves to whoever is behind me.

'Hey, Bet,' Flynn replies. He looks tanned and taut in head to toe workout gear; I wonder if he ever takes it off?'

'Hey, Flynn. Jake's just gaming at the moment, so you may have to knock extra loud for him to hear you over the zombies or whatever he's killing in there,' I say whilst shuffling around awkwardly trying to remain two metres apart from both of them in the narrow hallway. Flynn manages to step on the toe of my trainer as we both move forward at the same time. I lose my footing and cling onto the wall like an insane spider woman.

'Sorry, sorry, Alannah,' he says, talking into the back of my head. 'Actually, I'm here to see Bet and drop off these beauties.' Flynn's clutching a hand full of pink paper bags and looking pleased with himself. He looks so funny in his manly, black gym wear with his girly, little pink bags. I bet Becky ordered those. His arms are looking so toned, I bet Becky is loving life right now. My mind turns to Jake slobbing about on the sofa all day, every day and I sigh.

'Ooh, what is it?' Bet chirps.

'I've made some tasty protein balls for everyone in the balconies, they are guaranteed mood lifters so I'm just dropping a few off for everyone to keep their spirits up. Jake's already had some but here you go, have some more.' Flynn chucks a bag at me and I pathetically fail at catching it, watching it plonk down onto the floor. The brown balls roll out unenthusiastically. Everyone stares.

'Oh. Shit balls,' I curse at myself, annoyed for not catching them.

'No, they're dark chocolate protein balls,' Flynn mumbles, embarrassed.

'I bet they're lovely dear,' Betty titters as she takes one out of her bag, examining it as though it's a precious jewel.

'Oh, I didn't mean the balls are shit, I mean. . . never mind. How's Becky?' This is so awkward. Not seeing another man in the flesh up close other than Jake and my brother is clearly having its effect on me.

'Yeah, she's cool. We doing the quiz tomorrow?' His eyes fall to my dress. He looks confused. Probably wonders why I'm so tarted up to see Bet.

'Yep, definitely. Well I better go, see you later. Bet, let me know when you need more supplies,' I gabble, then run off embarrassed by my weird lockdown behaviour.

'I will do, dear, stay safe,' Bet calls after me. I hear Flynn start a conversation with Bet about still having her spare key from when he let the carpet men in when she was staying with her son. I scurry off back into my home/asylum and leave them to it.

'Hey, how's Betty?' Jake asks as I come through the door. He's showered and he's wearing jeans for the first time in weeks. He looks and smells lovely. The record player is playing old jazz, it sounds like Billy Holiday, my favourite. He's picked up his crisp crumbs and delicious smells are coming from the kitchen. Well fuck me, he's cooking.

'Yeah, she's good, have you got aftershave on?' I smile. This makes a very nice change indeed.

'Yes I do. Walk this way, milady.'

Chapter Five

Jake ushers me over to the dining room table which he's laid neatly with red cloth napkins and matching silver and red cutlery.

He pops open a bottle of prosecco, spilling a little bit on his (also bright red) shirt before pouring us both a glass. Our small, glass dining table sits alongside our big balcony window and above the balconies opposite, the view of the sky this evening is beautiful. It's all reds, oranges and pinks and I gaze at it dreamily, taking in the calmness. Jake smiles at me, acknowledging the view I'm admiring as the late evening sunset bounces off the table. I feel all warm, fuzzy and soon to be fizzy inside.

'What's this in aid of? A celebration?' I ask, as he pours us both a glass. He's using my crystal glasses. The ones we only get out for very special occasions. My stomach lurches with bubbles and excitement.

'Just celebrating us,' he says nonchalantly, sniffing and tossing his head to the side.

'Ahh right. Well, to us then.' We clink glasses and each take a sip of our fizz. The bubbles warm my mouth and instantly make me lightheaded.

'What are you cooking? Smells delicious,' I chirp, squinting my eyes at the sun. It's been a long while since he's cooked me dinner.

'Chicken a la Grecque, it'll be ready in about thirty minutes.' Jake bites his lip, he looks nervous. So sweet. I suddenly feel guilty about cursing him in my own head. He's not always a lazy couch potato incapable of doing any housework, just the last few weeks really.

'Oh wow, you haven't made me that for years, yummy, can't wait.' Jake used to cook it all the time when we first met, he went out with a Greek girl before me and learnt the recipe from her. It used to annoy me that he had to tell me that part but it doesn't anymore. Jealousy used to be an emotion that I felt often with Jake as girls were always chasing him, I haven't felt that for a while. Perhaps we've grown up a little, perhaps we're ready for the next step or next few steps.

'Yes, I know but you deserve it, babe, come here.' Jake pulls me up onto my feet and kisses me softly. The exact way he does it, reminds me of when we first met. Jake and I were only meant to be a bit of fun, but fun turned into friends with benefits very quickly. Then love surprised us when he went away for work for a few weeks and we realised how much we missed each other. We used to write each other letters, it was very cheesy, but lovely.

Nostalgia takes over and I'm right back in his flat almost six years ago after a drunken night out in Coolsbay. He'd asked me at the bar if I was a model and I'd laughed at him, telling him to take his beer goggles off before sashaying off in the opposite direction. Laura and I ended up in the only nightclub in Coolsbay called Prancers and it was certainly full of lots of those. It was inevitable that Jake would end up there too, it being the only nightclub in town. He strode over to me on the dance floor with big clumsy feet and a bottle of Moet. The bouncer got angry and pulled him to one side to give him an ear bashing before we joined Jake and Flynn in a private booth to polish off the bottle. Jake and I chatted and laughed all night before ending up at his flat. Flynn was so quiet, barely said a word, I think Laura ended up pulling one of the guys from the local kebab shop.

Jake leads me over to the bedroom, still kissing me and we stay there until Alexa tells us our time is up. Bossy cow.

Having worked up a ravenous appetite, my mouth waters at the prospect of food. That was the best sex we've had in a while and I want more, in fact come to think of it that is the only sex we've had since the beginning of lockdown. I'm so happy we're connecting again, in more ways than one.

'Wow, that was fun, so hungry now,' I pant, fanning my face with my hand, still hot from our bedroom workout.

'Sorry for being, well you know… not me,' Jake says quietly as he does his shirt back up. He sighs, and I reach out to touch his cheek as he continues. 'I've just been finding it quite hard being at home all the time. I guess I've been feeling low and didn't know how to say it or deal with it,' he admits.

'No, it's fine, we all deal with things in different ways and it's a very strange time for everyone. I've missed you being you, too. You can tell me anything, please just talk to me from now on.' I smile, moving both of my hands to touch his.

'Yeah, I will. Come on, dinner should be ready.'

♥ ♥ ♥

During dinner we devour the tasty meal and chat about what weird and scary times we're living in. We also discuss the prospect of starting a family and Jake is willing, he's actually quite excited by it. I'm so happy I could burst. He did say he's only twenty-nine so still very young but he wants to start a family with me. Soon. Ecstatic doesn't come close. I happily hum along to the music, scrolling through my phone, dreaming of our future baby while Jake clears up with Billie Holiday still playing softly in the background. He simply won't let me help so I'm enjoying sitting on my arse being waited on for once. Maybe Billie could be our baby's name. So significant, so romantic. And it's gender neutral so it could work for either sex.

'So, does all of this loveliness mean you're going to help me around the flat more?' I call out to him teasing in a jolly tone. Part of me feels stupid having to say it and risk spoiling our romantic bubble of an evening, but it needs to be said and what better time than when we're both chilled. Jake comes back from the kitchen with an enormous, expensive looking Easter egg and some strawberries and cream. He dumps them on the table then picks up the wine.

'Yep, I'll try.' He pours me some more wine whilst avoiding eye contact. Not the exact answer I was looking for but I'll take it for the time being. Don't want to spoil the mood completely. My phone beeps and I check to see a message from Daniel on our WhatsApp group with him, me and Lisa.

'Who's that?' Jake asks, peering over the table. He never usually asks. Maybe he's feeling a bit sensitive and insecure, hence the slobbing about and the moods lately.

'Just Lisa and Daniel, I'll reply later.' I smile, putting my phone on the windowsill face down. 'So, have you got any more plans to do those fitness social media posts you told me about?' I ask, staring into his beautiful blue eyes. Jake had plans to be the next Joe Wicks but I think Flynn beat him to it. This appears to have put his nose out of joint a little bit and is perhaps why he didn't tell me about the shit balls. Perhaps he's jealous of the effort Flynn is making and thinks he's a show off. I think Flynn's just trying to be nice and raise spirits.

'Yeah, I'm going to start, I'll start soon. I just need to set up the account so people can pay me. I hope they buy my class. It doesn't help that so many people are doing it for free when there's other people like me that need to earn a living to survive,' he complains, rubbing his forehead.

'I know, it's hard.'

'It's different for you, you still have a job and you have savings.' He pouts and looks out of the window.

'Yeah, but for how long I don't know, who knows what will happen. And *you* still have a job.' Jake's also been furloughed but he isn't making any extra cash from his personal training clients which did bulk his pay out a lot. He pokes his little paunch, then says,

'I think I may have to lose this before I record anything. Not exactly a good advertisement for fitness, am I?'

'That will take a week at most, it's nothing. You look great,' I reassure him. He could still do the posts. He's still in good enough shape.

'Anyway, you don't have to be topless, wear a t-shirt you tart,' I tease.

'I'd get more subscribers topless I reckon, that's what the ladies like. And men,' he says, thoughtfully looking out of the window.

Flynn comes out onto his balcony looking more ripped than ever in tiny little shorts and Jake rolls his eyes. Becky follows him out with her *Kim Kardashian* bum, in equally tiny shorts and top revealing her taught stomach. Jake stares, I don't blame him, I'm staring too. But not because they look like they've been chiselled by the gods. It looks like they're having a row, arms everywhere, very animated for the normally laid-back Flynn. They clock us watching, Flynn marches back inside with Becky running after him, her bum bouncing around like it's got a mind of its own.

'Yeah, I'm sure you would.' I laugh, ignoring the fact I've seen Flynn and Becky.

'Sex sells babe,' he says shrugging his shoulders with a little smirk, still gazing out of the window.

'So when do you think you'll start the posts, you'd be so good at it?' I ask, genuinely interested.

'I'm not sure, please don't put pressure on me.' Jake's expression changes to irritated, maybe even pissed off.

'Sorry, just do it in your own time. I'm just being nosey. There isn't much going on in my life at the moment so I suppose I'm more interested in yours,' I reply brightly.

Jake turns grey and his shoulders drop. He puts his head in his hands and starts to breath heavily.

'Jake,' I say gently. 'Are you okay?' He begins to cry. Just quietly at first, then the big sobs come. My heart breaks for him.

'It's Mum,' he finally manages.

'Oh God, Jake, what's wrong?' I get up from my seat

and put my arms around him. He's shaking.

She's got the virus. She's got the virus.

'She can't manage, she can't afford the bills. The house is going to get repossessed,' he says, with terror in his eyes.

Okay so not the virus, phew.

'What, why?' It's not like him to get so upset. I mean I know it's shit but there are ways around it, surely.

'They've made her redundant at the travel agents and she's only been there nine months so she's not entitled to anything.' He sniffs, eyes all red from crying, they now match his shirt. I offer him a napkin; he takes it and loudly blows his nose.

'Oh Jake, why didn't you say, how much does she need? We've got savings.'

'Yes, but they're really your savings,' he says, blowing his nose again. True most of it is, when we both sold our flats, I made a killing and he didn't. We bought at different times. The market was extremely low when I bought, it was just luck. Sheer luck, but he's always been slightly put out by it.

'No, it's ours, it's always been ours and if we need to lend your mum money then we will. How much does she need?'

'About Two-hundred-and-fifty-pounds a month.' He sniffs, wiping his nose again. The dye from the napkin has come off and smeared onto his nose.

He looks like a sad clown.

'Okay, that's fine. You know the supermarkets are taking on, I'm sure she could get temporary work there for a while but I'm happy to help until she gets back on her feet.' The words come out of my mouth before I can stop them. Shit, can we afford it? What if I lose my job? Then we really will need that money to pay our own mortgage.

'Thanks, Alannah, I love you babe,' he wipes his face with the napkin as the tears stop.

There's no going back now. My face is set in a fixed wide smile. I pray this doesn't go on for too long.

It will be fine.

'I love you too. Honestly, I can't believe you've been stressing about this all on your own,' I say, still smiling and shitting my pants at the same time.

'Just don't say anything to her about the money, Alannah, she would be so embarrassed.' Big tears start to roll down his face again and I squeeze him tight and whisper in his ear.

'Of course, baby, of course. I'll pay you so you can transfer it to her, she doesn't need to know I know.' Poor Jake. Judy isn't exactly proud, but I guess I wouldn't want it shouted from the roof tops either.

In bed that night, I scroll through my phone unable to sleep after tonight's events and finally read the messages that Daniel and Lisa sent during dinner.

Daniel: *How's lockdown going guys? Lance finally rang me, he told me the reason why everything is emailed now is because he spoke to Zeze and said he was too embarrassed to do a Zoom call ever again and fears for his mental health. He doesn't give a shit. He actually thinks it's pretty funny but we have him to thank for no more video calls. Yes!*

Lisa: *Haha go Lance! I am so thankful to him. It's great not to have to look at Cherry's smug chops but so sad we don't get to look at the eye candy that is Daniel.*

Daniel: *Lisa! I am definitely not eye candy, that's our mate*

Alannah's department.

Lisa: *Oh I SEE, Alannah is a gorgeous lady I agree but sadly she's taken.*

Daniel: *Yes I know, unlucky for me.*

Wow, how do I reply to that? A few crying, laughing emoji faces should suffice, the best go to emoji when you have nothing to say. I wince, Daniel doesn't fancy me, he must be drunk or just trying to deflect Lisa's flirts.

I scroll down my WhatsApp to see an old message from Judy, Jakes mum. I start to reply to her saying how sorry I am for her job loss but think better of it. I don't want to make her feel awkward and Jake did say not to mention it. He messaged her about the money as soon as we had the conversation and said she was so relieved and thankful to him. After a session scrolling through Facebook and reading copious amounts of sad stories about the virus and the NHS, I make a mental note to call Laura again soon. Must check on her and see how she is.

Chapter Six

5 weeks since lockdown – The prime minister has had the virus.

'Hello, you, how's my partner in wine?' I chirp as Laura accepts my video call.

I'm sprawled out on my duck egg blue chaise longue in the bedroom, phone propped up on the windowsill, all dolled up and with a glass of fizz. I'm pretending that we're on one of our nights out and these are our pre-drinks.

Those were the days. We were free.

The last few weeks have been a combination of hard, boring, infuriating, Groundhog Day and then a little bit interesting/exciting. After speaking to Laura a few weeks ago she said my idea about making face masks for the NHS was lovely but they have all the proper face shields now. Instead, she suggested I make scrubs, as they're going through more than five sets a day at the moment. So that's what I've been busy doing.

Laura told me about a collective called Coolsbay Scrub Hub, so I looked them up on Facebook and joined up, they supply all of the fabric and the patterns and I just sew at home. I think there are about ten of us altogether. Mum lent me her sewing machine. She got a bit tearful when I went to pick it up, it's the first time I'd seen her since lockdown. All I wanted to do was give her a big squeeze, it was really sad. Mum's usually a social butterfly, she was always going out with friends. She has Gary of course but the rule of only being allowed out for essentials and one hour's exercise and not seeing anyone other than those in her household has really got to her.

My sewing machine skills were a bit rusty at first, but with a bit of guidance from my lovely neighbour Bet – shouting instructions over the balcony – and a fair amount of unpicking, my scrubs aren't looking too bad. It's immensely therapeutic. More so because I'm helping towards something that matters and doing something that truly makes a difference for once in this lockdown rather than just sitting on my arse trying to complete every film and series on Netflix. Having said that, I'm pretty sure I've completed Netflix anyway so God only knows what I'd be doing without this. It's saving my sanity.

'Hey, you, you look nice, you're making me feel really ugly, wish I'd dressed up now.' Laura examines her face on the screen before taking a gulp of her rosé wine. In the background, beautiful canvases of the beach and one of a meadow hang proudly above her sofa. Laura painted them herself, a woman of many talents.

'You look fab,' I lie. She doesn't, she looks knackered but why would she look anything else. She's probably working sixty hours a week at least.

'I'm not too bad thanks, lovely. Better than during the first few weeks. The surgery is eerily quiet, all the patients have to wait outside to be seen. We go outside to collect them, but for some patients I've been seeing them in the street as some are afraid and don't want to come in. We also keep getting people with tooth problems, which is a massive strain. I don't know why there aren't more dentists open, I've heard it's lack of PPE but I don't know, it's all really vague. I think we have one dentist open for emergencies in the whole town, they're essential workers like us, and I know I'm being unreasonable when I say this but I feel like they've taken this as a sign to have a fucking holiday.' She huffs and shakes her head, then takes a huge gulp of her wine again.

'That's ridiculous, it doesn't make sense.' Must make an effort to floss more so I don't get unnecessary toothache and put pressure on the NHS.

'We're still short on doctors though,' she continues. 'The first few weeks were so stressful with house visits. Remember I told you about that meeting at the beginning, when everyone was in tears?' She takes another gulp of wine and I notice her hands look incredibly sore. Red raw and dry. If they look that bad on video, they must be worse in real life.

'Yeah,' I do remember that. At the start of the pandemic Laura told me that the surgery had a meeting regarding house visits and the like. All the doctors were in tears for fear of catching the virus and spreading it to their own families. Not only that but there wasn't enough of them to go out and see the patients who needed to be seen at home, which made them feel helpless and guilty. Coupled with not enough PPE it was extremely stressful. I think back to when lockdown started and *Emmanuel's* closed. The big Zoom call with Lance's hairy arse, having to let staff go and being furloughed. It doesn't really come close to how Laura's work has been and I feel embarrassed for stressing over my (trivial by comparison) worries.

'Well, it's a lot better now,' Laura continues. 'Don't get me wrong, it's still terrible when we get a case but we're slowly getting used to the new normal. We all have lunch together now and make a big deal of having something nice to eat. We also do a fun quiz or play a silly game to keep spirits up. Also, we're becoming rather good at TikTok dances. If nothing else, this has definitely brought us closer together as a team.'

'That's brilliant, it sounds like spirits are lifting, like you're adapting to the big changes,' I say brightly, stroking my chaise longue. Since Boris Johnson has recovered from Covid, I think it has given people a little more hope. Perhaps things will be back to normal by June.

'Yeah, it is. Oh Alannah, I'm going to get so fat with all the food donations. Pizza, chocolate and cream teas galore, we've got them coming out of our ears. I'm in no way complaining as it cheers us up, but it's doing nothing for my jelly belly. You'll have to make me some super-size scrubs.' She giggles. But if anything to me, she looks slimmer.

'I'll make sure they're extra trendy though, you'll be the best dressed practitioner in the surgery.'

'Yes please. I want ones with newts on. Anyway, enough about me. How are you?' she asks eagerly.

'Newts? You're strange. Yeah, good, it's just same shit different day for me but so happy I'm making the scrubs and making some sort of difference.'

'It's so sweet you're doing that. Yes newts, they're my most favourite amphibian. Ever,' Laura says with enthusiasm but it's the first I've heard of it. She's one of those people who has a different passion or obsession every week and I can't keep up with it. When we went travelling, she went through a stage of only eating cheese and tomato sandwiches for weeks, then it was banana milkshakes substituting every drink. If those things weren't available, she simply wouldn't eat or drink anything. Rather extreme, but she's an all or nothing kind of gal and that's one of the many reasons why I love her.

'You're strange,' I say. 'Almost as strange as Beau and his love for slow worms. Yuk.' A memory of Beau pops into my mind of us as kids digging in the back garden, when he discovered his first ever slow worm. I screamed and heaved. He was over the moon with excitement. He's one of those people who has his favourite animal on everything. T-shirts, pillows, mugs, you name it. Slow worms aren't the easiest to find on those types of things so he often uses an old photo and gets it printed on said products himself.

'Don't diss the nature, miss. Anyway, how's it going your end?'

'Not too bad I guess; we've got a little community going on the balconies. Quite a few of us take part in a weekly quiz which is fun but it can get overly competitive between Flynn and Jake. Everyone helps each other out with food, so if someone can't get something, we just message the group and it appears on your door step a day or two later, as if by magic. And I'm buying for my neighbour, Bet, as she's been told to stay home.'

'Ahh, that's so nice.'

'Yeah, it is nice, there are worse places I could be locked in. I don't have a garden but I have the beach on my doorstep and a balcony to sit on. It definitely could be a lot worse.'

'Definitely. And how's Jake?' She mouths Jake's name without sound, I'm guessing in case he's eavesdropping but she needn't worry as he's probably in the living room fighting off zombies again. I mouth back *annoying* whilst miming a gun shooting me in the head, before doing my best zombie impression. I feel slightly harsh when Laura starts giggling and snorting but since he asked for help with his mum, he's turned back into a lazy bastard again.

It's really starting to grind my gears.

After our lovely dinner and heart to heart about life and the revelation about his mum a couple of weeks ago, Jake partly got his arse in gear. He phoned Flynn and got some tips on how to hold successful gym classes online. To my surprise he's out filming himself on the balcony right now, the curtains are closed but I heard him welcome people to his virtual spin class. I'm not really sure how that can work without a bike but I daren't ask.

I say partly got his arse in gear because the flat is still a fucking dump. He really doesn't seem to care. There have been a few discussions about it, he says he needs to focus on the classes and making money, I said well, that's great but can we also focus on not living like stinking pigs. I am so bored of the sound of my own voice. At this rate we won't be starting a family as he is the biggest child I know. If I have to pick up one more wet towel off the bedroom floor, I swear I will smother him with it.

Not to mention the countless coffee cups dotted around the entire flat that just sit there, growing mould, perhaps he's seeing if he can grow the elusive vaccine for the coronavirus and then he'll surprise me with it and save the entire nation. 'Sorry, sorry babe that's what I was working so hard on, I couldn't tell you as it was top secret. Now, let's buy that mansion you've always dreamed of and a cleaner for every room,' he'll announce, just as I'm about to suffocate him with said towel.

I've half given up myself really.

Susie, our cleaner is very much missed but even she wouldn't pick up his towels so why am I doing it all of a sudden?

'Babe, I'm done now. I'm just going to grab a shower.' Jake comes in from the balcony sweaty and red in the face with a towel around his neck. I still don't know how he did a spin class. Maybe he meant something else.

'Okay, why don't you wait five minutes, it's the clap for the NHS tonight, it'll be starting soon,' I remind him.

'Nah, they can't hear me, can they?' He scoffs and wipes his forehead with his already wet towel. No doubt another one for me to pick up later. Urgh.

'It's not about whether they can hear you, it's to show support. Comradery,' I explain. Actually, Jim at number nine does work for the NHS so that's at least one person who *will* hear.

'Come againery?' Jake laughs his donkey bray laugh and stomps off to the bathroom. My blood boils. It isn't always like this. It's just the little irritating things that are magnified to a thousand percent when it's just the two of you, day in, day out and NO ONE else.

People are starting to come out onto their balconies, so I walk out onto mine and wait. I'm surprisingly excited by the prospect of seeing all my neighbours. Bet is sitting on her balcony, admiring her hanging baskets and sipping a small glass of sherry. My other neighbours are a quiet couple, whose names I've recently learnt are Donna and Dominique. They sneak out onto their balcony and offer me the same small identical smiles they do every week. Complete with matching hair styles, they could easily pass for cousins at least. It's funny how some couples seem to morph into each other. A disturbing imagine pops up in my head of me sat on the sofa in Jake's stained jogging bottoms. It makes me shudder; I definitely like my hygiene and nice dresses too much.

Beau is waving frantically from his balcony in his baggy yoga trousers and I wave back with the same franticness before he starts speaking to his neighbour, Pat, who has a pet parrot. Beau and I speak all the time, but I still miss hanging out with him. Before all this, we would always go to gigs together and attempt surfing. The latter was always funny with Beau, usually because he was as high as a kite and had no control over his balance whatsoever.

Flynn saunters out onto his balcony in nothing but a pair of tiny black shorts, but Becky hasn't appeared again, she hasn't been around much lately. She also hasn't been present at the weekly virtual quiz for a while. Flynn said she's having to do her own family quiz with her parents and sisters, and it clashes with ours. I offered to change it, it's not like we have any other plans or anything but he said not to bother as she isn't one for quizzes anyway. Maybe she just doesn't like us. She isn't really my type of person anyway, whenever we saw her and Flynn, she never really said much and when she did it was all about herself. I'm not really sure what he sees in her apart from her impressive buttocks.

Everyone's clapping now. There are a few wolf whistles and cheers as we continue to slap our hands together. The clap goes on for a good five minutes before everyone begins to chat across their balconies. A woman from a few balconies below begins to sing a song she's made up about the virus, it's awfully depressing and her voice is equally as awful. It's interesting how everyone wants to showcase their non-talents at the moment. Must be sheer boredom and loneliness taking over, causing people to become extremely deluded.

I'm such a lockdown bitch.

'Alannah, how's it going? Where's Jake?' Flynn shouts over the woman's awful singing.

'Yeah, alright thanks, still sewing scrubs and trying to make myself useful. He's indoors, think he's killing zombies again now, want me to get him?' I shout back, just as the woman screeches out something about dying all alone in pain. Jesus Christ.

'No, no, I wouldn't want to distract him from that. What a shit not joining in.' Flynn grimaces.

'I know,' I agree and roll my eyes.

'That's amazing, what you're doing. I wish I was that talented.' He runs his fingers through his dark, wavy hair. The singing woman appears to have finished her song and I hope that's it now. No one cheers and I wince. I think she's got the message that she hasn't got through to the next round of *Balcony's Got Talent*.

'Oh, it's not talent, just gives me something to do.' I smile and blush at the same time, despite myself. Why does this man never wear any clothes? It isn't even that hot.

'You should make something for you, it can be your

work bonus to yourself.' He grins while I try to remain focused on his face and not his incredible abs. What a pervert. I glance down and to the side to avert my eyes and notice the man in the maisonette to the left of the flats standing in his garden. He's bald and also topless, wearing bright yellow shorts, his podgy belly highlighting Flynn's God-like torso.

'Yeah? I might make myself a new nighty out of this funky fabric,' I joke, pointing to the pink, blue, yellow and green patterned scrubs hanging on my washing line. Great, I bet I've conjured up a beautiful mental image for him there. NOT.

'Maybe not a nighty, I think only my gran wears them.' He laughs again, looking shy.

The guy from the maisonette is busy filling up his watering can with the hose. For the first time ever I'm jealous and wish I had a garden. He waters the stunning flowers with great care, taking his time on every single plant. That must be a nice hobby.

'Yeah, we'll see,' I reply to Flynn, thinking he probably thinks I wear old granny nighties now. 'Where's Becky?' I'm not really too fussed where she is but I want to change the subject from me wearing a granny nighty as I now feel at least eighty years old.

'She's having a lay down, headache I think,' he says looking past me.

I'm just about to ask him if everything's alright when out of the corner of my eye I spy maisonette man again, he's moved to the little alleyway down the side of his house, probably thinks he can't be seen. It all happens so quickly; he pulls his pants down and crouches down over something as I gawp in horror. What the actual fuck am I watching?

I furtively look back at Flynn who's already leaning

over the balcony trying to catch a glimpse of what I've spotted. With exaggerated finger pointing and wide eyes, I signal for him to look into the garden. Maisonette man, is now in a most uncompromising position. Flynn opens his mouth, gobsmacked, then covers it with his hand. Maisonette man appears to be holding a tube, no wait, is that the hose? He's also pulling the weirdest of faces. Flynn and I look back at each other, we're both thinking the same thing. We continue to watch on in a mixture of horror, disgust and amusement as the man stands up and proceeds to ram the hose right up there. Christ he'll wash out half of his internal organs at this rate.

'Mate I've got toilet roll if you need it. No need for an outdoor bidet,' Flynn shouts, totally out of character. It makes me jump and my jaw drops. 'Do you not have a bathroom you can do that in?' he carries on. I duck down so maisonette man doesn't see me peering through the wrought iron balcony bars. Maisonette man looks up and sees Flynn. Startled. He drops his hose, with the water spraying everywhere, quickly pulls up his yellow shorts and scuttles off back inside his house. Flynn is laughing, bent over and holding his stomach.

'Why did you do that?' I shriek, tears rolling down my cheeks. Hysterical and struggling to breath, I'm still crouched down for fear of maisonette man seeing me somehow. I must look completely insane.

'Why not?' He laughs. 'I couldn't resist, he was washing his bum in public, the best bit of entertainment I've had in weeks. Thought he could use a hand.'

'He was quite happy with his hose, I think.' I shriek again, then clasp my hand over my mouth in case there's a chance he can hear me. We both roll around on our balconies laughing and crying at the same time until Jake's voice booms out.

'Babe, keep the noise down, I'm on level ten now and I can't concentrate with you idiots laughing.'

Chapter Seven

7 weeks since lockdown – 10ᵗʰ May - People can go out all day and meet with one other person outside of their household. Some people can go back to work but not all.

'Well, what do you think?' I ask Jake. I'm standing in front of the TV blocking the zombie apocalypse that's been taking over our flat for almost two months.

Jake's slouched on the sofa, in his grey jogging bottoms and grey t-shirt, with what looks like tomato ketchup stains down the front. Alluring.

'About what?' Jake groans as he leans to the side to kill whatever's behind me. It infuriates me. I press my lips together, trying to keep my cool and stop myself from exploding.

'Notice anything different?' I try again, smiling brightly. I'm standing here in my new homemade dress; I consider doing a little twirl but think better of it as I might block another zombie murder.

For the past two weeks I've been busy beavering away on my dress in the evenings whilst Jake does his own thing which mainly consists of killing zombies and balcony workouts. I've only been sitting at the dining room table every night making this and bunting for our flats' communal VE day celebrations but I may as well have been in an entirely different universe. I seem to be totally invisible to him at the moment.

'No but, babe, you're kind of in the way here,' he says leaning to the other side, fingers working at full speed on the games console.

I'm absolutely fuming.

I huff and turn on my heel, stomping off down the hall to our bedroom. I slam the door like a moody teenager who's been grounded indefinitely then look at myself in my antique mirror. My face is screwed up and doesn't suit the dress so I try to rearrange my expression into a smile but it looks more like I'm straining for a shit so I go back to a half neutral, half scowling face.

I'm so proud of this dress, I've never made anything like this before. The fabric is light and airy with an intricate flower pattern. It was by no means easy to sew either, matching the fabric was a complete nightmare, not to mention the movement of the fabric itself. If I make another one, I'll definitely choose something easier. I've worked my arse off and he doesn't even notice or care.

Still looking in the mirror, I grab my phone from the bed and snap away. Before I know it, I've uploaded a photo to social media of me posing in my new frock. Shameless. It's something I would never ever normally do, post for likes, but I need a confidence boost. Instantly it receives likes and comments, including a message from some fashion blogger wanting me to make her a dress and a matching facemask so she can sell it for me. Yeah right, how cheeky? Nice try, lady. I imagine Jake seeing it and ignoring it before he goes and likes some photo of a perfect model posing in a bikini. This makes me seethe even more so the photo gets sent to the group chat I have with Lisa and Daniel along with a bunch of other people with the caption 'made it myself' underneath it. I get an instant reply.

Daniel: *Wow, you look absolutely stunning. Can't believe you made that.*
Me: *My own fair hands. Thank you, glad someone thinks so.*
Daniel then messages me privately.
Daniel: *Beautiful. Who wouldn't think that?*
Me: *Maybe the man I live with, he hasn't even noticed.*
Daniel: *You're joking me? Well he's an idiot.*
Me: *I wouldn't go that far but he has his moments. How are you?*
Daniel: *I'm good, been working on a song about the NHS.*
Me: *Really?*

Part of me cringes as I think of the woman below belting out her depressing creation every Thursday night, but the other part is wildly curious as to what he has put together.

Me: *Sing it to me.*
Daniel: *Hmmmm really?*
Me: *Go on, it will cheer me up.*
Or perhaps not, I hope it's not too depressing.
Daniel: *Okay, wait. I've actually recorded it, so I'll send you the video.*

My feet tap excitedly on the floor as I sit on the bed waiting for the video to download. Daniel appears, sitting with his guitar, wearing a white t-shirt and black beanie hat. Dave the cat is walking along the back of the sofa behind him, waiting for his moment to steal the show I expect. He strums away and I like the tune, it's funky, almost has a rock feel to it and the chorus is really catchy. But it's his voice. His voice is like creamy, nutty chocolate, all rich and gravely. It's got me weak at the knees.

The kids are going crazy and the house is in a mess, I wish I could go out but this is for the NHS.
Lockdown baby
Sitting on the sofa
Lockdown baby
Just checking out the fridge
Lockdown baby lockdown
My work has got me furloughed and I'm bored as I can be, I wish I could go out but this isn't about meeeeeee.
Lockdown baby
Tidying me house again
Lockdown baby
Just chucking out old shit
Lockdown baby lockdown

It takes a second for me to realise that this is a piss take when it cuts to him scoffing food from the fridge, feather-dusting his house dressed as Freddie Mercury from Queen, chucking out old clutter and eventually hurling his cat outside. He's even got some kids running around causing mayhem in a split screen. That part amuses me. Too busy swooning over his voice to notice sooner, I begin to laugh, this *has* cheered me up.

Me: *I love it, it's hilarious.*
Daniel: *It was fun to make, those kids are my nieces, I haven't stolen any kids for the making of this video. My sister*

sent me the clip.
Me: *It's really funny, got any more planned?*
Daniel: *I might do a song about a beautiful maiden trapped in her castle, wearing her own handmade clothes.*
Me: *Isn't that the story of Cinderella?*
Daniel: *Haha, yes you're right, okay back to the drawing board.*

Footsteps thud down the hall, I instinctively turn my phone off and chuck it in my handbag before busying myself with tidying my dressing table. I shouldn't be feeling so guilty. Daniel only said my dress looked nice.

'Babe, have you seen my phone?' Jake asks as he walks into the bedroom stroking his new best friend, tramp beard. I really hate beards and he's been growing one since lockdown began. This last week, it seems to have doubled in length and girth and it's beginning to look as if a white and ginger guinea pig has taken up permanent residence on his face. Laura once told me that an average man's beard has more germs in it than a toilet seat. Revolting.

'I last saw it over there on the floor.' Where you leave everything else, I think. He slopes over in his stained joggers and picks it up.

'Ah yeah, there it is. I need to message Mum back, a woman that she used to work with has the virus and she's really ill.'

'Oh no, that's awful. Is she in hospital?' Shit, this is all becoming a bit too close to home. Poor woman. Laura only messaged me last night to say that another one of her patients had died. It's so incredibly sad.

'Yeah, she's in intensive care. Mum doesn't know her well but is really upset. She's also worried she may have got it from her as she's not been feeling right,' he says, looking down at his phone.

'That is really sad, but your mum will be fine, she got made redundant at the start didn't she so she's been away from work for well over a month so she would already have had it by now.'

'Oh yeah, yeah she will be fine, you know what Mum's like, worries over nothing,' he says, scratching his nose.

'Has your mum had any luck with getting a new job yet?' I ask. There's only so long I can continue to fund her.

'What is it with you?' he mutters, still staring at his phone.

'Sorry?'

'What is it with you?' he repeats slowly as he looks up and stares into my face. His eyes aren't the usual bright blue I'm used to staring back at, they've turned dull, like they have a mist or fog set over them.

'What do you mean?' I say slowly, narrowing my eyes and matching his tone.

Jakes face turns puce. A disgruntled white and ginger guinea pig.

'All you do is moan and complain and now all you're worried about is getting your money back. Mum might have the virus. Do you even care?' he barks so loudly it makes me jump. He never raises his voice like that.

'Of course, I care,' I spit back, both surprised and annoyed by his temper.

'Well act like it then.' He snarls through gritted teeth as he tosses his hair out of his eyes. This makes my blood boil.

'How fucking dare you. How dare you say I don't care. I wouldn't have helped if I didn't care. I don't think it's unreasonable for me to ask what your mum's up to. Maybe I should message her, I'll get more sense out of her than you. And the reason why I moan and complain as you put it, is because I'm constantly picking up your fucking shit and I've had enough of it,' I bite back, with angry tears burning down my cheeks.

It's all coming out now.

'What do we have to tidy up for? It's not like we can have people over anymore. Mum doesn't need any more pressure, so don't message her. She doesn't need the extra worry. Just don't pester her,' he shouts. This is probably our first shouting argument in the whole time we've been together, we've never really argued. Jake's always been so easy going and usually we laugh about stuff or discuss it properly but we never shout and scream at each other. Never.

'You're pathetic and lazy. I'm sick of picking up your festering stinking towels and disgusting protein wrappers and crisp packets stuffed down the side of the bed. Do you know what I found the other day? Your dried-up bogies smeared underneath the bathroom sink. Revolting,' I rant, almost heaving from the memory of them. 'Fucking vile,' I continue. 'And when you actually have a shower, how about picking up your own wet towels,' I screech at the same time picking up a towel he has previously left on the floor and chucking it at him. The stench of damp wafts past me as it flies through the air.

'You don't give me a fucking chance to tidy them up,' he says   catching the towel and dropping it on the floor again. 'You're scurrying around after me as soon as I've dried myself and it's so irritating. Just. Fuck. Off,' he bellows before stomping off out of the bedroom. I hurl the towel at him again and it lands on the back of his shoulder.

'Maybe spend a bit less time playing your pathetic teenage zombie game, and you might actually have a little more time to clean up after yourself and not be such a dirty revolting slob,' I roar after him.

'Fuck off,' he repeats, peeling the towel off his shoulder and throwing it back at me with such force that it almost knocks me over.

'Use this to clean your rancid bogies off, disgusting prick.' I hurl the towel back at him and it lands perfectly on his face. Grabbing my handbag off the bed, I run past him out of the door as he mutters obscenities under his breath, the towel still on his head.

I need to go on a long walk, a really long walk. I just want to stay out and never go back. I feel as though I'm living with a stranger. Who was that in there? Not the Jake I know, and I don't recognise myself either. I really wish I could see another person, it's so intense, just the two of us.

I've given up watching the news, it's way too miserable, all you hear is virus, virus, virus, death, death, death. But I still follow the updates so I know what I'm meant to be doing and don't unintentionally get arrested. Yesterday, Boris announced that you could meet with one other person who isn't from your household as long as you social distance. Relief washes over me as I remember this, and I make the decision to see if Beau is home. It will be so good to see him in person.

I march over to his flat and he answers within seconds. I gasp. I hardly recognise him. His usually long scraggly hair is all gone and is now clipped short at the sides and longer in the middle like a Mohawk, it's a bit of a home do bodge job but it looks better than it did before. But it's his eyes that look the most different, they are clear, not bloodshot anymore.

'Wow, Beau, who's given you a makeover?' I say, surprised by his appearance. I want to hug my brother.

'Hey, sis, nice to see you, man. Yeah, the new barnet, I got bored of brushing it, man,' he says, looking pleased with himself. 'I was just about to go out though.' He strokes his new hair up into a point in the middle, which I'm pretty sure he never brushed anyway.

'Don't worry. It's just Jake and I had a horrible row,' I say, bursting into tears like a nervous wreck. 'I don't know what's happening to us. He's a completely different person,' I howl into my hands.

'Oh, sis. I was meeting a mate, but I'll cancel, we can chill at the beach. I think you need it,' he says, reaching for his phone in his pocket.

'Are you sure? I feel bad for ruining your plans,' I say, blowing my nose on a crumpled tissue I've found in my handbag.

'No, no of course, she'll understand,' he says, tapping away at his phone. He gets an instant reply, smiles, then replies to her again before putting his phone back in his pocket.

'To the beach.' He points towards the sea before stepping outside and closing his door.

Beau and I stroll down to the beach while I listen to him chatting away to me about meditation and cleansing his chakras with crystals. He's totally given up the cannabis which makes me so proud of him, and is living a much more wholesome, drug-free life. Although he then admitted to having one last session when Batshit Steve managed to get hold of some and dropped it off to him a few weeks ago. His last little treat. They got super high and rapped along to Snoop Dogg on video call for three hours. I hope he doesn't do that again, it would be all too easy to get back into that bad expensive habit, he isn't the type of person to just enjoy the occasional joint, it has to be several, every night. Beau says he can get me some crystals that will help with my mood and self-love. I'll take anything at the moment. We sit down and I make swirling patterns with my fingers in the sand as Beau listens to me bend his ear about the stress with Jake, his moods and slobbishness, and the fact that I stupidly agreed to lend his mum money until she gets another job, whenever that might be.

'Hmmm, don't take this the wrong way, sis but he couldn't be liaising with another lady, could he?' Beau raises his eyebrows in question.

'I don't think so, why? It would be nearly impossible to do that at the moment, wouldn't it?'

'You'd be surprised what people can get up to, not everyone follows the rules,' he says, raising both eyebrows. 'Batshit Steve has been outperforming home visits to a handful of ladies.'

'Gross, he has a girlfriend.'

'Exactly.'

'No, he wouldn't have the time, he's always at home, he doesn't even go shopping.'

'Yeah, but *you* go shopping,' Beau counters.

'No, no, he wouldn't, he couldn't,' I defend the man who is making me miserable.

'I'm just saying, don't rule it out, man.' He puts his hands up in the air. 'Maybe just ask him, no harm in asking.'

Chapter Eight

The next day

It's shopping time. The time of the week that I categorically dread. I normally try to go as late as possible, to avoid the queues, but this time I've opted to come early. I'm shopping for Bet as well and I need to deliver her stuff as soon as possible. I've been stalling for a few days after my argument with Jake so it's my own fault and now I'm having to rush about like a headless chicken.

I pull up to the supermarket in my car and groan as I see the queues, it's 7.30am and there's already a long queue of people standing outside with their trolleys, waiting to get into the shop. There's no turning back now, the next supermarket is at least twenty-five minutes away so that's a no go. I put on my yellow flowery mask and get in line, making sure I'm two metres behind the person in front. I'm instantly joined by someone behind me who is not keeping their distance, so I turn around and give them a steely look that hopefully says *stay back*. It works and they shuffle back a bit before I turn back to face forward. My yellow flowery mask obviously means business.

Finally, I enter the store, spray down my trolley and hands then let out a big sigh as I take a look at my long list. I let out an even bigger sigh when I read Bet's obscure requests. I'm pretty sure they stopped selling half of these items in the 1980s, but I shall try my best.

I do my utmost to follow the arrows around the store. It irritates me when I see other people not bothering, then I realise I'm doing the same thing and I have to do a quick glide and reverse to go the right way again. Never has shopping been so stressful. I wonder when we'll go back to some sort of normality. Trash TV helps me feel normal, it's a much easier and happier place to be at the moment.

'Alannah, Alannah!' Hearing my name being called in a supermarket is kind of a regular occurrence in Coolsbay. This is the only supermarket for miles, so you're always bound to bump into someone you know but it still puts me on edge as it's super awkward if the other person wants to chat, it just isn't really possible anymore. You aren't supposed to get close to anyone so how can you have a conversation? But it's the voice that puts me on edge more. I instinctively try to hide behind the flowers, maybe I'll blend in with my mask. I really don't feel like talking to anyone today. I pretend I haven't seen her, but she clocks me peering out from behind the orchids. I perform a series of faces from confusion to shocked, to show that I've *just* noticed her and definitely wasn't ignoring her. I hope it's convincing and I don't look too much like a constipated goldfish – at least it's only my eyes showing my expressions.

'Hi Zeze, how are you? I didn't think you lived around here?' I say, emerging from behind my camouflage, smiling brightly inside my mask. In fact,

I'm pretty sure she lives well over an hour away.

'I'm looking after my mother, she's local. She's had a nasty fall so I'm staying with her for a while. How are you coping? You're still looking really thin,' Zeze says, openly judging. Looking me up and down, up and down, until her eyes finally rest on my face.

'I'm doing fine thanks and I'm just naturally slim, no need to worry,' I reply, nonchalantly, while fighting the urge to tell her how fat she looks. She looks as if she has gained around two stone of lockdown lard. I console myself with the fact that I'm generally a nice person, resisting the compulsion once more to be insensitive back. 'How are you?' I ask.

'Not so good, I've been furloughed too now. Alannah, I don't know how long we will keep our jobs for. *Emmanuel's* is in trouble. That is my honest opinion so I would say to you now, off the record, start looking for something new.' She puts her hands on her hips and frowns.

I'm not sure what to make of this. Is the company folding or is this just Zeze's speculation? Does she just want me out? Want me to find a new job so I won't need to come back?

'Thanks, Zeze, but I think I better wait to hear it officially. Wouldn't want to start looking and then word get back to *Emmanuel's* as that wouldn't look good would it?' I want her to reassure me. She doesn't.

'Suit yourself, but don't say you weren't warned,' she says, abruptly.   'I better go, Mama is waiting and she gets cranky if she doesn't get her snacks on time,' she continues, looking me up and down again.

'Okay, Zeze, see you soon,' I call after her sweetly as she waddles off towards the crisp isle. The sad thing is I will probably take her advice and see what job opportunities are about, but I don't want her knowing that, just in case. You can't be too trusting these days, perhaps I should message that fashion blogger back, desperate times.

I skate away in the opposite direction to Zeze, heading towards the egg aisle. My mind returns to my conversation with Beau, settling on the word *trust* as Beau's voice echoes in my head, *maybe just ask him, no harm in asking.* I shake the thought out of my head, there's no way he could be cheating but if he's going to do it, he would be doing it right now, wouldn't he. When I'm not there. An image of Jake in our bed with another woman, who weirdly resembles Becky, flashes in my mind.

He could be doing it right now.

Lost in my own torturous thoughts, I almost skate past the eggs. I thought panic buying had stopped but there's only one pack left. The new trend seems to be baking which of course requires plenty of eggs.

My Facebook feed is full of people making the not so appealing, boring banana bread which mostly looks so heavy and leaden I imagine it's like swallowing a slimy, sugary brick. There are also a lot of delicious looking cakes, tray bakes and chocolate treats on my feed. I won't be baking but my mouth waters anyway thinking of chocolate treats as I grab the last pack of eggs. But I can't get them to my trolley, there's a force stopping me. The force is another hand pulling on the other end of the egg box. Well this is awkward. I look up to see who this hand belongs to and a woman, about my age, with long brown hair scooped up into a ponytail, stares back at me. Her hand still gripping firmly on the pack of eggs. Glaring.

'These are mine, get your hand off them, they're

going to break,' she squawks, glaring at me with squinty bitch-eyes. How rude, if she'd asked politely then maybe, but absolutely no way now.

'Hmmm, these are actually mine, I had my hand on them first,' I reply, still ensuring that I don't loosen my grip on the eggs or take my eyes off her.

'You're going to break them. Just let go,' she raises her voice and gives them a sharp tug. The muscles in her arm and shoulder flex, she's strong. My weak-muscle, noodle arm is no match to her toned guns but I'm not giving in.

'No, you let go,' I spit, tugging back and narrowing my eyes.

This is war.

'Seriously, you're going to have to let go,' she whines through gritted teeth, tugging at them once again.

'No, these are mine, and anyway you've come down the aisle the wrong way so that makes your claim invalid,' I snarl, surprised at my own reply. I usually hate conflict of any kind but I'm feeling so angry I can't help myself. The row with Jake has had quite an effect on me.

'Let go,' she snaps.

'Absolutely not,' I say slowly. I realise I'm smiling and if it wasn't for the mask I'm hiding behind, I'd look like a complete psycho. I may still look like one, but I don't care. Not one little bit.

'LET GO,' she shouts and tugs, her ponytail swinging from side to side. The eggs are probably broken now anyway but that's no longer the point. It's survival of the fittest.

'ALANNAH! CHESKA, is that you? A familiar male voice breaks our dispute and we both look up to see who it is. We're both still gripping firmly on the eggs.

'Flynn, long time no see,' she simpers, then smiles, what I imagine to be a wide smile behind her mask, showing off perfect teeth. I notice she has beads of sweat on her forehead and I'm happy I've given her a good fight. A small boy of about four or five-years old peers out from behind one of Cheska's legs as she ushers him forward. I can't believe I didn't notice him before; he's not made a sound.

Suddenly this all feels very wrong.

'Do you know her?' I ask Flynn, incredulous. 'Here, have them,' I say politely to Cheska, letting go of the eggs.

Someone had to give in. If I'd seen the little boy earlier, there would have been no fight.

'Thanks, it would have been easier if you had done that...' she starts.

'Yeah, we used to work together,' Flynn cuts her off and I continue to glare at her. Don't push it lady. He looks awkward. Oh God, don't tell me this was a past fling or something.

'Many years ago,' she says, fluttering her eyelashes at him.

'All okay now?' Flynn asks carefully looking at Cheska and then me. I nod slowly and Cheska's eyes smile. 'This lockdown is doing crazy things to all of us isn't it? And what's your name little man?' he says, expertly smoothing over our spat. I'm suddenly very aware that a small audience has gathered around us. Flynn sees me clock them and motions for people to leave by waving his hand forwards and they do, even if reluctantly.

'That lady was mean to my mummy,' the little boy moans, ignoring Flynn's question, whilst pointing at big, bad wolf me. 'Mummy is making me a birthday cake and she needs the eggs to make it for me and that lady was trying to steal them,' he continues, pouting.

Oh great. Now I'm the evil villain. I blow air out of my cheeks, feeling the proverbial egg splat all over my face. I wish I could fly back home immediately with my new evil villain cape. Egg Monster.

'I'm sorry, I hope you have a lovely birthday. How old are you going to be?' I say sweetly to the little boy, desperately trying to redeem myself.

'Five and you're not invited to my party,' he pouts then sticks his bottom lip out.

'Well no one can have parties at the moment, can they, mate? But I'm sure your mum will make it very special for you,' Flynn says gently to the little boy.

The boy nods and smiles before hiding behind Cheska's leg again for a sly nose picking. Crotch goblin should have made himself present a lot sooner, he could have saved us all this grief.

'Anyway, ladies, I better go. This isn't the best place for a chat. Cheska, nice to see you again, you're looking well, and Alannah, I'll see you tonight for the quiz?' Flynn asks with a little grin. I imagine Cheska pursing her lips together, seemingly not pleased that we know each other well.

'Yep, Jake's not coming though so it will just be, me, you and Beau.' I reply, basking in my own familiarity with Flynn. I'm so thankful that he's here, God knows what would have happened if he hadn't been. A flashing image of the little boy swimming in eggs and cracked shells on the shop floor buzzes into my mind's eye as I imagine I'd taken to smashing them over his mum's head.

Cheska holds down her mask and mouths a *thank you*

to Flynn before she whips her ponytail around and grabs her little boy's hands with one of hers whilst holding the eggs in her other one. She offers a small wave to Flynn and a disdainful look at me, translated as *fuck you* as she skooshes off against the direction of the floor arrows.

I narrow my eyes and watch her saunter away.

'You alright?' Flynn asks. He lunges forward to touch my arm then remembers the rules and pings back into place. 'Oooops,' he says, shuffling from side to side, chuckling.

'Yeah, just embarrassed,' I say with pink cheeks, smiling at Flynn's awkward dance.

'Don't be, you did the right thing, giving her the eggs. It's not worth it.'

'Yeah, I couldn't really not give them to her, could I. How can I take away a child's birthday cake, even if he was a crotch goblin?'

Flynn's face erupts from behind his mask into a huge grin before his shoulders start to shake with silent laughter. He then closes his eyes, bends over and lets out a big, warm, hearty laugh and I can't help but burst into laughter along with him. It was rather ridiculous, never in my life did I envision that I would be fighting a stranger over a box of eggs.

The rest of the shopping takes over an hour to complete as I spend most of my time searching for Bet's requests. I can't complain, she's so lovely and bakes Jake and I a nice homemade pie or crumble every week, leaving it on our doorstep. She doesn't have to; I'd shop for her anyway without question. There's a strange moment where I think I see someone strongly resembling Jake's Mum working on one of the tills but as I march over to take a closer look, she's swapping shifts with someone else and leaves.

Out in the car park, I rip off my mask, load my bags into the car and drive home. My heart's in my mouth as I put my key in the front door, my overactive mind paranoid at what I'll find. As I walk into the living room, Jake is on his phone texting, he's still ignoring me after our fight. After today's drama I'm really ready for another fight and this time I'll make sure I win. I whip round the back of him with the shopping and do a sneaky peak over his shoulder as I take it into the kitchen. He's talking to Flynn.

'Hello, have fun shopping, did we?' he says, looking up at me, smirking. Obviously, it's worth talking to me now he can poke fun.

'Yes, it was wonderful,' I say sarcastically, dumping the shopping bags down on the floor. Flynn's blatantly told him about my showdown in the supermarket and I feel slightly betrayed that he's done that.

'Didn't know your mum had a job in the supermarket,' I say in an attempt to take the focus away me and onto someone else.

It probably wasn't even her.

'Oh yeah, I've been meaning to tell you about that,' he says rubbing his tramp beard. 'She's just got the job but the pay is so low and the hours aren't very many so she will still need a little help for a while. Is that okay?' he asks, and I sigh inwardly.

'How long have you known?' I reply, feeling the anger bubbling inside me again.

'She's only been there a few days, I wanted to tell you but you were angry at me and I was trying to give you space.' He jumps up off the sofa and surprises me by pulling me into a big bear hug.

I start to cry, today has been a shit one. I don't know

if I have a job anymore, I've stooped to an all-time low of fighting with strangers in supermarkets and my own boyfriend thinks all I do is moan and complain.

It's a pity party for one.

'I'm sorry, I hate it when we fight,' he says into my ear.

'Me too,' I reply, sniffing into his shoulder.

'So, tell me about your scrap in the supermarket, I want to know all the juicy details.' He grins and I roll my eyes before telling him all the gory details, yolks and all.

Chapter Nine

10 weeks into lockdown – 1ˢᵗ June – 6 people can meet outside under new measures to ease lockdown. Non-essential shops are due to re-open on the 15ᵗʰ June.

The smoke alarm rings in my ears as I wake up to the smell of Jake cooking what smells like a fry up. He's okay at cooking but he always seems to burn a fry up.

No doubt my birthday breakfast. I'm starving and despite the fact I know what's coming, my mouth waters. I roll over in bed to check my phone for birthday messages and see messages from Mum, Beau, Lisa and forty other people on Facebook who I never see.

I haven't had a present off Jake yet and he doesn't do cards, I expect he'll give it to me when he serves me my burnt breakfast in bed. He's been making a bit more of an effort over the last few days and I'm glad I didn't take Beau's advice and ask him if he was cheating, that would have really caused a horrible atmosphere of mistrust. I'll just put it down to the fact we're going through a bad patch. It happens in the best of relationships. I'm sure ours isn't the only relationship suffering during lockdown.

'Breakfast for milady,' Jake announces as he brings in the fry up on a tray with a glass of orange juice and a cup of tea. As expected, the bacon's burnt and the eggs look solid but I don't mind, it's the effort and thought that counts.

'Why thank you, wow this looks tasty,' I lie, giving him a kiss on the cheek.

'Just like me.' He grins and I notice the crumbs in his beard. 'Oh, I almost forgot, your present.' He jumps up, then digs around in his drawer before he pulls out a small gold wrapped box with a dark gold bow. This looks like a nice box, a box that could have a ring in it. Before lockdown my stomach would have been somersaulting with excitement at the thought of finally getting engaged. Now, my heart is in my mouth. It's not the right time. We still haven't discussed the baby thing again and I feel like that needs to be addressed before anything else. I'm not even sure it's the right time to try with all this uncertainty over our jobs and everything else that's going on in the world. But when we discussed it, we left it pretty open, as though it was going to happen soon.

'Oooh, what could it be?' I say, smiling nervously. Jake, grins back at me and flicks his hair out of his eyes. I open the box but there's no ring. Slightly disappointed yet relieved all at once, I delve around in the box's padding and pull out earrings. They are not to my taste at all; big and clunky with loads of bright colours.

They're parrots.

He got me parrot earrings.

They look like something an eccentric old lady would wear to a wedding. I swallow my dissatisfaction.

'These are lovely, so bright, thank you.' I smile my

well-rehearsed smile. I'm used to getting disappointing presents from Jake, he just isn't very good at buying what I like. I'm not going to spell it out for him as it would just be like I'm placing an order. A gift shouldn't be that; it should be thought of by the person buying it. So, I tell myself to be grateful, grateful that he took the time to choose them and thought I would love these brightly coloured parrot earrings, even if they are the epitome of vile.

'Glad you like them, babe. Anyway, I'm off to finish my game. I've only got one more level to go and then I'm done. There's a new game coming out soon, so I want to complete this before the launch date. Enjoy your fry up.' He grins then bounds off down the hallway whilst I gulp down tears of frustration and anger.

I haven't got the energy to argue with him. I don't want to be a martyr. The old me wouldn't complain about him having to do gaming on my birthday but the old him wasn't a gamer before all of this so I didn't need to. I feel guilty for feeling so unhappy and angry that he can't wait to play his stupid game on my birthday. I lie in bed for a bit longer, pulling myself together and cheering myself up by focusing on deciding what to wear. I'm going to dress up and make a real effort to feel special.

I *will* have a good time even if Jake has nothing planned. I've already lowered my expectations and am guessing he hasn't arranged anything; he'll use lockdown as an excuse anyway so I can't get any more disappointed than I already am. He's done his burnt fry up in bed so he thinks that's his get out of jail free card to play zombies for the rest of the day.

I'll arrange a video call with Beau and some friends

later, that'll cheer me up. I've eaten the bacon and eggs and I'm picking at the burnt sausages, chewing each mouthful carefully so as not to break a tooth when our doorbell rings. The property management company still haven't fixed the main door and intercom, even though I've reported it several times. I'm guessing that's been put on hold along with everything else. Quickly, I throw on my dressing gown to see who it could be. Low and behold Jake is still gaming when I pad past him and he makes no attempt to move.

'Hi Judy, this is a nice surprise,' I say, opening the door to Jakes mum. 'I wish I could invite you in.' I pull a face, standing there in my dressing gown. Still not dressed at 11am, feeling like a birthday tramp.

'Don't worry, love. I won't stay long. 'I've got work in a bit. HAPPY BIRTHDAY. I hope you like it,' Judy sings and points to a huge box she's left on the floor. And when I say huge, I mean enormous.

'Wow, you didn't have to do that,' I say. She really didn't have to do that. The poor woman has barely got a new job and now she's spending her wages on me.

'It's a TV,' I exclaim as I pull the wrapping paper off. It's a forty-inch TV. It must have cost what I give her a month at least as it isn't a cheap make either. I stare at it, trying to act pleased but feeling completely bewildered.

'It sure is, I thought you could use one for your bedroom. Jake told me he's gaming a lot so it means you can escape that rubbish and watch what you like, whenever you like.' She beams and blinks, nodding her head, her brown curly hair bouncing around her face.

'That's so lovely of you, Judy, thank you, it's really great. You shouldn't have,' I reply warmly. You really shouldn't have Judy.

'Well you know, with the new job and the redundancy… '

'Mum! What are you doing here?' Jake bellows in my ear, making me jump. She looks mortified, his poor mum.

'Oh, nice to see you too, son! I thought I'd surprise the lovely Alannah on her birthday actually, thank you very much. I'm not here to see *you*.' She composes herself, grins and winks at me, Jake forces his way out in front so he's blocking my view of Judy. The shit.

'Mum, what the? What's that?' he asks, pointing at the TV box, exasperated.

'What does it look like? It's a TV for Alannah, so she doesn't have to put up with all your crap all the time.' She laughs, dismissing his dramatic reaction.

'Mum, you can't afford that,' he exclaims.

I laugh too now, but partly because it sounds like his voice is breaking.

'How do you know what I can afford? Mind your own business. If I want to buy my daughter-in-law a TV, then I will.' Judy smiles, and puts her hands on her hips. Defiant. She insists on calling me her daughter-in-law because she doesn't know why he hasn't proposed yet either. She's called me it for years so neither of us bat an eyelid now but when she first started doing it, it was very awkward. Jake did tell her to stop and she told him *never*.

'Sorry, Mum, you know I just worry about you, how's your friend? The one that's ill?' he asks, frowning.

'First time for everything,' she mocks. 'She's okay now, out of intensive care and on the mend, she should be home soon but of course will then have to self-isolate for a while. She'll be fine, thank the Lord.' Judy crosses her hand over her head and chest and kisses the cross that's hanging around her neck. It makes me smile; I've missed Judy. 'Well I best go, got to get to work now,' she says as she looks at us both expectantly.

'How is work going? Jake hasn't told me much.' I dig him in the ribs as he's entrenched in front of me now and all I can see is his big sweaty neck. I peer out from behind him and I swear he starts to pull the door shut; I firmly shove him to the side so I can see her better. He always reverts back to a child when his mum is around, but this is a whole new level. Perhaps it's magnified because he hasn't seen her for so long. Most things seem exaggerated and intense during this pandemic, feelings, bad presents, future worries.

'Yes, it's going well thanks, love. I'm really enjoying it, it's nice not to struggle so much anymore. Thank you,' she replies and I assume she's saying thank you for the money, perhaps she's worked out that it's me lending it to her and not Jake, even though it's coming from his bank account.

'Oh good, I'm glad you're enjoying it and no problem. Well let's catch up soon. I feel like I've hardly spoken to you.' I glance at Jake whose neck is getting red and blotchy.

'That would be lovely, let's do that.'

We say our goodbyes and watch her go before Jake picks up my giant TV and we go inside.

'Why are you acting so weird?' I ask, as soon as the door closes.

'Shhhh,' he says. 'She'll hear.'

'Hardly. That was so rude, trying to close the door on our conversation, what's wrong with you?' I almost don't want to know the answer. Maybe he is having an affair and his mum knows and she's bought me this TV because she feels sorry for me and this will be my new companion when he leaves. He says nothing. I wait a beat, giving him a chance to reply. He doesn't, so I continue, 'I take it we can stop paying her now that she can afford this?' I point to the TV and Jake just stares at it.

I glare back at him, waiting for an answer.

'Yeah, of course, yeah, we can stop paying her now,' he mumbles, looking at his feet, then gazing longingly back at the sofa and his game. I tut and roll my eyes, but he doesn't seem to notice.

'Okay good, that settles that then.' I huff, slightly surprised at his reply.

I'm sure he said she needed the money for a few more months but I'm not going to pursue that, and Judy seemed pretty content with her new job so I'm not too worried.

'Right, I'm going to get in my party frock then, it is MY birthday after all,' I announce before swanning off to the shower.

Today *will* be a good day, even if I have to force it.

I spend hours getting ready and thoroughly enjoy it. I have a long shower, wash my hair, then carefully remove my Chewbacca lockdown fuzz. It's been highly neglected for the last few months – I now own a blunt shaver. Next, I enjoy a soak in the bath and use a bath bomb I got for Christmas but hadn't got round to using until now. The colours swirling around in the bath send me into a kind of hypnotic trance and I just lay there, thinking about everything and nothing until my fingers are so wrinkled that they feel like they belong to someone else. Finally, I heave myself out of the bath and stomp down to the bedroom.

I've already decided what I'm wearing, it will be one of my own creations, a red and white striped tea-dress with short sleeves, pockets and white star shaped buttons down the front. When I twirl, it spreads out around me like a flower and I feel a million dollars in it. I blow dry my hair so it has maximum volume. It's grown far too long for a bob now, but it settles nicely just above my shoulders into a soft wave. Slapping on a full face of makeup, my war paint for the day, I finish off my look with the brightest red lipstick I own. My phone buzzes just as I'm thinking about whether I should wear the parrot earrings just to please Jake.

Laura: *Happy Birthday my lovely, I hope you have a wonderful day. What have you got planned? By the way I was wondering whether you would make me a dress? I am obsessed with the one you posted on Instagram with matching facemask! My sister also wants one, obviously I will pay you!!! Just tell me to do one if you don't want to, I'll completely understand.*

Me: *Thanks so much mate, I miss you. I would love to make you and your sister a dress, no charge for you, it will be a gift but I'll have to charge your sister if that's okay. Not much planned today unless Jake has a surprise in store.* And I very much doubt that.

Laura: *I'll call you tonight if you have no plans and I insist on paying for my dress as well.*

Me: *Call me now if you're free? We can discuss dress material over a glass of wine, exciting!*

Laura: *Haha wine! It's only 1pm but it's 6pm somewhere right? Ringing you in five, grab the vino…*

Laura rings and we spend over two hours putting the world to rights and designing her dress. Bet told me I have quite a talent for dress making which made me feel very humble. She's been examining my pieces on the balcony; we almost have an unspoken arrangement to meet and discuss my sewing every day. It's so much fun and I can tell Bet is just so pleased for me. She's been a great motivator and often dishes out little pearls of wisdom. My favourite Bet quote being; '*difficult roads often lead to beautiful destinations Alannah, and in your case, beautiful dresses.*' She keeps me going when I doubt myself and feel like giving up. I'm still sewing plenty of scrubs for Coolsbay Scrub Hub, but dresses are my passion.

Laura tells me about a dance she's organising for everyone at the doctor's practice to perform. They've already done one dance but want to keep going with it as it's good for keeping spirits up, especially as one of the doctors thinks he has moves like John Travolta from Saturday Night Fever. Laura says he actually looks like a turkey taking a shit. We both end up snort laughing down the phone to each other, until we realise, we've both sunk an entire bottle of wine each and decide it's time to go. After the phone call, my head is spinning and I'm feeling rather drunk now. The only option to feel better is to flump on the bed and close my eyes. I wake up, disorientated and with no idea what the time is. I've got a thumping headache and a mouth like a badger's arse.

Jake's standing over me with a massive bunch of beautiful flowers.

'Wow, what a nice surprise, they're beautiful thank you. I did wonder if the parrot earrings were a joke,' I croak, rubbing my eyes, still feeling slightly drunk.

I catch sight of myself in the mirror and let out a groan. My freshly blow-dried hair and immaculate makeup are no more. Red lipstick is smeared all around my mouth and chin, mascara down my cheeks and hair like a parading, male cockatiel. Wow, I actually look very much like Pennywise from the film IT, it's quite uncanny. At least I would know what to do if I went as him to a fancy-dress party. A good costume idea for Halloween.

'No joke. These aren't from me,' he snarls, dumps the flowers on the bed and leaves.

Chapter Ten

It's the morning after the night before and my head is pounding as I wake up realising, I'm still wearing my clothes. I lift my head off the pillow with much effort and look in the mirror. I flump back down, not wanting to see that state again. The sight that stared back at me looks very similar to yesterday's Pennywise after my afternoon nap and drinking session with Laura. Not pretty.

Jake's already up, he has a PT session lined up, apparently. I stupidly check my phone and see an ominous email from Emmanuel's, it's Manni the director and the title of the email reads *future plans*. My stomach turns over and a huge sense of panic starts to ripple within me. It will have to wait until I have recovered from this second mammoth hangover. I can't deal with any more surprises right now. Beau's right, I am getting too old for this shit. Last night, I was thrown the most memorable lockdown birthday party ever by some of the loveliest people in my life. I just want to stay in my little bubble and carry on reliving those memories, just for a little bit longer, before I have to face reality.

♥ ♥ ♥

Last night

'Beau's at the door,' Jake bellows from the living room. I fall off the bed and drag myself to the front door to see my brother. I still haven't eaten anything since the burnt breakfast and I feel like I'm going to be sick.

'Sisss happy birthday, oldie! Thirty-two and looks like poo. Fuck. What have you been taking? Don't be starting drugs now, you're way too old for that shit.' Beau laughs, his hands in his pockets, looking at me with mock concern. Jake scoffs then looks at me in disgust before sloping back off to the sofa.

'Urgh, no way, just wine. I had wine, lots of wine with Laura on a video call and now I feel like death,' I moan, sounding like a camel with a sore throat. Beau's wearing his colourful yoga trousers, a white t-shirt and an amber beaded necklace, very rainbow rhythms. He's way too chirpy and zen for my afternoon hangover.

'You look like it too. Myyy precioussssss.' Beau proceeds to leap around on all fours doing his best Golem impression. It's times like these when I want to punch him. 'Christ on a bike.' He laughs and gets up. 'You look so rough, how's the birthday been so far? Pretty good by the looks of it,' he giggles.

'Thanks, we've established I look like shit. Yeah, it's been okay,' I say glumly.

'Just okay, did the big man not spoil you?' Beau says loudly so that Jake will hear.

I'm past caring, we had a blazing row about the flowers and the parrot earrings, I still don't know who the flowers are from. It'll probably be Lisa and she forgot the card, which reminds me I really need to finish her dress and matching facemask as I'm seeing her soon. Why did I promise to make so many dresses for people? Think I got just a little over-excited. I shake my head and make a face that says don't even go there. Thankfully, Beau gets the hint.

'Anyway, I came round to tell you to be ready on your balcony for seven.'

'Why's that?' I don't think I can stomach any more balcony bingo or any more wine for that matter.

'You'll see,' he grins.

'Shit, it's six already. I need to eat too!' I screech, half excited, half wanting to vomit. I hope I get a second wind.

'Eating's cheating,' he chirps.

'Right, I better go then, I'll see you soon.' I slam the door shut and scuttle off into the house, stuffing two brioche rolls in my mouth from the kitchen cupboard before attempting to sort out my car crash of a face. I spend way too long examining the new wrinkle that's appeared on my forehead and wonder if lockdown has aged me or if it's the aging that has aged me, either way it's depressing. Is now the time to consider a bit of cheeky Botox? I couldn't even if I wanted to as everywhere is bloody closed. An hour later and I thank the lord that I don't resemble something that looks like the walking dead anymore. Fresh face, hair and dress and I'm ready for round two. Pass me the vino. It doesn't really matter how much I drink or if I get a hangover as I have nowhere to be. I'm a lady of leisure now, Livin La Vida Lockdown.

I pour myself a glass of champagne in my hardly ever used crystal glass, the last time we used these glasses, Jake and I were planning our future. I've decided I'm treating myself on *my* birthday, I did pick up the wine but put it back down again when I spied the champagne. This was a gift from my mum for moving into our flat. We were saving it for a special occasion. Obviously, we didn't have any of those or we would have drunk it by now, I think, bitterly.

Stepping out onto the balcony, I gasp as a huge round of applause ripples around the other balconies. I almost walk into the giant pink shiny balloons bouncing around on my balcony. How on earth did they get up here? Everyone is out on their balconies in their glad rags and is raising a glass to me. There's bunting on pretty much every flat and it's not the same bunting I made for VE day a few weeks ago either. Beau is on his balcony honking a massive comedy horn, Mum is at the other end of his balcony jangling a tambourine and side stepping along to the music.

I want to cry when I see her face, my lovely mum.

Flynn is out on his balcony playing what looks like a penny whistle and the lady from below is belting out "Happy Birthday" on her brand-new microphone which is a lot louder than the last one while everyone else sings along. Bet waves at me, she's wearing a glitzy dress, sipping her sherry and looking so glam. Donna and Dominique are out wearing matching smart tuxes and with their matching hair styles. They both raise a glass to me, flashing their identical smiles. The song finishes and Bet disappears then reappears on her balcony carrying a gorgeous cake covered in strawberries and cream with a pretend candle on top. I pretend to blow it out but still make a wish of course, wishing for the same thing that I wish for every year… a baby.

Old habits die hard.

'Wow, thanks Bet, that's so sweet. My favourite.' I beam, taking a sip of my champagne and admiring my cake, then take in the views of the colourful people, balloons and bunting. I smile at Bet and wave at everyone, feeling like a princess, or the Queen.

'It's no trouble dear. You look lovely Alannah. Beautiful dress, did you make that one?' Bet beams back at me and I want to squeeze her so much. Perhaps I should make Bet something, apart from what she's wearing today, all her clothes are looking so baggy these days. A nice twee tea-dress would look so sweet on her.

'Oh no, not this one, this is from Emmanuel's,' I reply, feeling a sense of dread as I speak the name of the company that I so-say still work for. I'm still furloughed but what Zeze said in the supermarket has been playing over and over in my mind, what if the company is folding? I shake that thought and try to concentrate on enjoying myself. No time for that right now. 'Anyway, let's talk about your dress, it's gorgeous. You have quite the figure, Bet.'

'Thank you, Alannah, I used to wear it to cocktail parties in the 80's.' Bet's eyes shine as she smooths down her dress. 'You could have fooled me and said you'd made yours; you have such a talent Alannah and I really mean that. I've been sewing for years so I know what I'm talking about; you really do have a skill. I couldn't make those style of dresses you're making anymore,' Bet says with a wobble in her voice.

'Thanks, Bet, that means a lot. I still feel like such an amateur.'

'You know what they say, every artist was first an amateur. Where's that young man of yours?'

I open my mouth to reply but I'm thankfully saved by the doorbell, so I excuse myself and make my way to the door. Jake is keeping very quiet and has made no attempt to see what's going on, come to think of it, I didn't notice him when I came out onto the balcony. I walk through the flat to the front door and don't see or hear him, perhaps he's gone out or perhaps it's him at the door and he forgot his key. Can't even bear to be near me on my own birthday.

'Flynn,' I squeal, opening the door. 'Have you come to serenade me with the tin whistle?' I tease. He laughs uncomfortably and looks down at his feet. He's dressed like a posh waiter; white shirt, black bowtie, black trousers and shiny black shoes.

'I've made some chocolate balls, or shit balls as you like to call them and you'll be pleased to know they aren't the healthy kind,' he says, his cheeks pinking up.

'Thank you and what's this?' I point to the tray he's balanced on his other hand.

'Ah, these are some little canapes; cooking has become my new found hobby.' He smiles to himself and looks over at them proudly, cheeks still pink. His long, dark horse-like eyelashes curling slightly at the ends. Why do men always get the good eyelashes?

'Listen, why don't you come in? The balcony is large enough to social distance, you can sit one end and me the other. I could do with some company,' I offer, giggling, the champagne's making me giddy and going to my head already.

'Is it allowed? Well I guess the politicians are hardly setting examples themselves, let's face it,' he replies thoughtfully, then nods his head. 'Alright,' Flynn answers.

'Exactly, come on in,' I chirp. 'Just pop the trays down on the table outside. Glass of champers?'

Flynn nods again then cautiously enters my flat after I step out of the way, remaining two metres away from him. Then I watch, transfixed, as he glides across the living room with the trays up in the air, above his head, trying desperately not to touch anything. He makes it looks so elegant, like he's doing some kind of salsa dance. He turns and twists this way and that way, winding his hips around the sofa and dining room table like a trained athlete, still keeping his trays high up in the air above his head. His arm muscles bulge under his white shirt with the weight of the trays. My eyes, distracted by the impressive hip movements, move up to his face, which is turning redder with every step he takes.

He's holding his breath. Protecting himself from *my* germs?

Flynn reaches the balcony and slams down the trays on the table, puce face and gasping for air, he leans on his knees to catch his breath back. A shit ball bounces off one of the trays and lands on the floor with a loud plop.

'Sorry,' he pants, out of breath, 'I'm only used to holding my breath for short periods, I do it all the time in the supermarkets when people get too close,' he continues, huffing and puffing.

'I could tell, that was quite the effort just to come out onto my balcony.' I laugh then take a sip from my champagne. I'm glad he holds his breath in other places too, I was starting to feel a bit dirty. I take another sip of my champagne and it goes down the wrong way as it fizzes up my nose, making me snort and sneeze into my elbow. Definitely not elegant. Definitely thinks I'm dirty now.

'Yeah, sorry.' He stands up, ignoring the pig noises coming from me, 'I must have looked like a right idiot.' Quite the opposite what I'm really thinking, he looked graceful apart from the pink face, it's not usually a word I would use to describe a man but that's the word that describes him perfectly. Like a graceful gazelle.

'Jake not here?' Flynn asks, interrupting my thoughts of a gazelle with Flynn's face, galloping across the desert.

'I don't know where Jake is.' I fill up his champagne glass then slide it over to his side of the table. 'We've not had a good day but the less said about that the better,' I whisper, just in case he's in here hiding somewhere. I glance over at Bet and she's talking to her next-door neighbour about being stuck in the house all the time. Flynn looks uncomfortable again. Damn, this champagne is letting out the evil truth-demon.

'I've been meaning to ask you something.' Here I go again. 'What made you text Jake about my argument in the supermarket with that Chesky woman?' I raise one eyebrow, hoping I sound matter of fact. I'm still annoyed about it.

'I just wanted to check you were alright, Cheska can be a bit feisty and Jake knows that so I told him to check up on you.' He looks at me with almond shaped, amber eyes, the same colour as beau's hippy necklace. It's strange I'd never noticed before, perhaps it's the champagne and the sun enhancing the colours. My pink balloons are rather bright too.

'I can hold my own too, you know,' I say, fluffing my hair and puffing out my flat chest.

'I know you can.' He smiles. 'It wasn't that, I was just looking out for a friend that's all.' He smiles again but with more teeth.

'Thanks, I think, so how's things with you?' I top up our champagne glasses again. Flynn opens his mouth but then the sound of someone playing a saxophone interrupts our conversation.

We peer over the balcony. Beau is down on the patio playing one of my favourite Club Ibiza songs "Save Me", Mum's down there too, shaking her maracas. And Laura. Laura is playing the beat on the bongos. I catch her eye and we laugh. I keep laughing until I'm hysterical and tears fall down my cheeks at the same time. I turn to Flynn and he grins then starts dancing so I join in and before we know it, everyone is out on their balconies dancing and swaying to the music. Since when did Beau play the saxophone and how did I not hear him practice? The woman below starts singing and I wonder if it's rehearsed or if she just knows the song, either way it actually sounds amazing. Hairs stand up on the back of my neck and I never want this night to end. Beau plays a few more songs, we eat a few more shit balls and canapes, drink a lot more, then finally when the older neighbours have had enough and mention that they are turning in, Beau, Flynn, Laura and I head down to the beach.

Beau and Laura end up skinny dipping in the sea, both as mad as each other, as Flynn and I chat about the pros and cons of lockdown, work and relationship strains. Flynn opened up and confessed he's worried about Jake. He said that apart from the text about Cheska, Jake hasn't responded to any of his other messages and phone calls. They were so close before all this, always out training and socialising together, Flynn said it's like he's become a totally different person and is worried about his mental health as Jake's suffered from depression in the past. Really? This is news to me. It then dawns on me that Jake could be really suffering mentally with all of this. Have I been a complete bitch to him?

I've suddenly sobered up, coupled with a bad taste in my mouth.

I just want to go home.

Flynn and I meander back to the balconies, leaving Beau and Laura behind to frolic in the sea. We say our goodbyes before returning to our respective flats, then my phone beeps as I turn my key in the lock. I creep in the door then watch Jake asleep on the sofa for a few minutes, I touch his shoulder but he doesn't stir so I pad down the corridor and fall into bed. I have no idea when Jake got back, where he's been or if he even knew about the party, either way I feel sad that he didn't join in and that I upset him. He must think I'm so ungrateful, I'll wear the parrot earrings tomorrow when I speak to him. My phone beeps again, it's probably Flynn checking I got home okay.

Daniel: *Hey, happy birthday beautiful. I hope you had a great day and liked the flowers, let's meet up soon xxx*

Chapter Eleven

Dear all,
I hope you and your families are keeping safe and well in these unnerving and uncertain times.

The days have flown by since we closed our stores at the end of March, hoping we'd all be back to work and normality after a couple of weeks. I must start by apologising for not updating you sooner but we wanted to have a fixed idea of where the business was headed first. Initially, we acted fast and cut staff costs which has done a little to help but no way near enough. As you all know the furlough scheme has now been extended to 31st July and will continue thereafter until the end of October, but from 1st August companies will be required to make a further contribution towards salaries which we are not in a position to do. It is sadly very clear that we will have to make many more significant cuts in order for the company to survive this pandemic.

Whilst I appreciate that at the start of this pandemic, I promised there would be no cuts to management staffing levels, I'm afraid I was wrong. I was so very wrong and I am so very sorry. I can no longer promise anything at Emmanuel's. We now need to act swiftly and decisively for the benefit of all and I'm afraid that this will have a personal impact on many of you. I'm sorry to be the bearer of bad news, but I feel it best to be open and honest with you.

The future plans for Emmanuel's will be to predominately sell online. It will be no mean feat as we don't have a great online presence at the moment but it's something we have been strongly advised to do and are currently working on; therefore, all of our stores will close apart from a select, carefully chosen, five. We need to all pull together and focus, I'm asking you as managers to think outside the box and submit your own business plan along with a short paragraph of what you bring to the company.

The area managers will also be scoring all managers in their region in areas that include skills and experience, standard of work performance, attitude to work and attendance and discipline. We will have just one area manager to oversee the remaining five stores. Your score will be taken into account along with your business plan and character paragraph and those with the best attributes will be selected to manage the remaining stores, the rest will be selected for redundancy. Of course, you may wish to volunteer for redundancy, however I'm afraid there is no extra money in the pot to reward those for doing so. We will pick one store manager per region which means the successful applicant will travel no more than ninety minutes each way to the nearest remaining store.

Please send in your business plan and character paragraph by noon on Monday to HR. In due course, you will receive an email from HR with your score advising if you have been successful or not. If you have any questions, hopefully these will be answered in the follow up email from HR later this afternoon.

Giovanna joins me in sending her best wishes and I look forward to hearing all of your innovative ideas very soon.

Many Thanks

Manni

Shit.

My phone says its 10:45am, which means I have precisely one hour and fifteen minutes to submit my grovelling *please pick me* email along with my innovative *Dragon's Den* idea.

Not going to happen.

Lisa. She'll know what to do. I grab my phone and start typing a WhatsApp.

Me: *Lis, I've literally just read the email from Manni, what the hell?!*

Lisa: *I have been stressing about it all weekend. I didn't want to message you about it as it was your birthday and thought you'd have it all sorted anyway. I've just finished mine now – I'll forward it to you.*

Me: *No don't. We are competing against each other. It wouldn't be fair. I don't know what to do!*

Lisa: *Shit mate. I don't know what to suggest apart from you better get cracking!*

Me: *You're right, chat later. P.S Did you know Daniel sent me flowers?*

Lisa: *I may have given him your address . . .*

Me: *You are one naughty lady.*

Lisa: *I know.*

♥ ♥ ♥

I sit on the sofa for fifteen minutes just staring at Manni's email. My mind is completely blank. There are no great marketing ideas for the company floating around in my head, not one. And I wonder if the lack of inspiration is because I don't really care anymore. If I'm totally honest with myself I haven't done for a while. Being on furlough and not working there has made me realise how much I don't miss it. I've worked there for over seven years so I would get *some* redundancy money if I was to be made redundant and I still have some savings which makes me think the next thing I need to do is broach the money subject with Jake regarding his mum.

I'm not paying her anymore but I want what I've already paid her back. I need it, even though I've finally had the refund from our holiday to Sardinia, it just went straight back onto my credit card and paid that off. Do I really want to go back to Emmanuel's? If I didn't go back, what the hell would I do? Retail is all I really know, it's all I've ever done but I must have *some* transferrable skills. Surely.

There's now forty-five minutes left, so instead of getting on with the business plan, I do the sensible thing of working out how much redundancy money I would get. Not too bad, it would last me around six months if I'm very careful. I stare at the screen for another five minutes then scroll through my phone for a further five minutes or more. The fashion blogger pops up on my news feed and I'm sucked in, scrolling through all of her posts showing her wearing gorgeous outfits, reading all the lovely comments that people have posted on her outfits. They're all asking, where they can get one too? I think, what have I got to lose and send her a message whilst biting my now overly chewed bottom lip.

Hey, it's Alannah
You messaged me a few weeks ago regarding the dress I'd

made and posted on Instagram and asked if we could work together. I wondered if you were still interested in receiving a sample and advertising it on your Instagram? Here's the photo of my dress again to remind you. Xx

I'm not sure what I'm wishing to achieve here but I'm desperate and it's worth a shot. She reads the message but doesn't reply and I sit there with the time ticking by, just staring at my phone, willing her to reply and chuck me a lifeline. It's been a while since she messaged me. Perhaps I've missed the boat and she is so in demand that she doesn't want to promote me anymore. I've either missed my chance or I'm very naive and it's a fake account that just contacts people for free dresses, then you never hear from them ever again.

With twenty-five minutes left. I reluctantly start typing my email to HR. What I'm typing is probably utter shite but at least it's something and I'll stand a chance with something, rather than nothing. I suggest bringing in a new section that will appeal to those going back to work and applying for new jobs, a business-wear section that is sleek but not too expensive. Alongside that I suggest we revamp the events wear to cocktail garden party dresses and have the mannequins in the window sipping on their cocktail Quarantinis or Locktails, so we are, in effect, displaying a quarantine after-party, like life after the American prohibition.

I'm sure the people of Coolsbay will be throwing large parties when this is all over. Showcasing their new found baking and cooking skills along with showing off their laborious home improvements and brand-new landscaped gardens. I explain that the weddings should stay as they are, this is a major part of our business anyway and it will always be busy but we should focus on parties and work for now. I finish the email off with a bit of sentiment as I really mean it, this is a sad time for the company. Manni is a good person to work for and even though I hardly see him, he treats the staff well and it's so sad to see the business that he built from scratch go from flourishing to having to be completely rethought and rebuilt again. He must be devastated.

Now I'm in the flow, my character paragraph is surprisingly easy. I list my achievements at Emmanuel's, pointing out that my store has been one of the top five stores since I started managing it. I'm a dedicated, friendly, fair manager who always gets the best from her staff. After I've finished, I read it back. I may just be in with a chance, if I want that chance.

Email sent.

The front door slams, making me jump, seems like Jake is back from his personal training sessions. He's been out all morning. I had to move his pillows, dirty pants, tissues and duvet so I could sit on the sofa this morning as that's where he's been sleeping.

'Hi,' I offer, whilst jangling my head so he can see the parrot earrings. We still aren't talking but I'm not one to ignore him completely. I actually really hate conflict.

'Hey,' he mutters, marching past me to the kitchen where he grabs himself a drink and an energy bar then marches into the bedroom. Twenty minutes or so later he returns, showered and changed out of his gym wear.

'Going anywhere nice?' I ask, because he's shaved his tramp beard off. He looks so different. Like the old pre-lockdown Jake who took pride in his appearance. The Jake I knew and loved.

'No, just out.' He takes one look at the parrots and walks out of the front door, slamming it behind him. Charming. He makes me so fucking angry. He was the one who bought me this shit, thoughtless present and didn't join in on any of my birthday antics, sulking in the living room like a moody teenager for the entire night. He's been the one acting like an utter arsehole for the last few months and yet he is treating me like I'm in the wrong. I rip out the parrot earrings and throw them in the kitchen bin. Then, despite myself and feeling guilty, I take them out again, heaving at the slimy potato skins that are touching them. I give them a rinse and carefully place them on the side, poor ugly parrots.

I force myself to muster up the energy to go for a walk. I need to clear my head and figure out what the hell I'm going to do with my life. In all aspects of it. I message Beau to see if he wants to join and he replies saying he'll meet me in an hour at the beach as he's with a friend. I can't wait that long. I need to go for a big stomp now but I message him back to say that's fine as I'll just meet him after.

I take a brisk walk down to Emmanuel's; I haven't been anywhere near it since it closed but I feel the need to see it right now. It feels so good to power walk and with every stamp on the pavement I imagine myself getting closer to clarity. There are lots of people about outside as it's a nice sunny day, people nod and say hello, I smile and say hello back. It's nice to see people. Joggers and bike riders swish past in their Lycra. The more I stomp, the better I feel and before I know it, I'm running, running in my flipflops like Phoebe from *Friends*. Limbs everywhere but I don't care, it feels so good. The town centre appears in my vision in the distance and I slow right down to a stroll to take in the eerie ghost town.

Everything is closed. As expected, but it still hits me.

I stroll up to the little toy shop and peer in through the shop window, it looks just the same as always apart from the fact that the lights aren't on. My eyes are drawn to a morose looking doll that's been sitting in the front window for years. It stares back at me with big, sad, watery eyes, making me shiver. I carry on past the pasty shop, jewellery shop, a seaside shop that sells souvenirs, buckets and spades, and a small boutique that sells retro vintage clothes, before finally arriving at Emmanuel's. The bakery opposite looks sadly frozen in time with a faded poster advertising Mother's Day in their shop window – so long ago. I wonder if they'll survive. All these businesses are small and independently owned.

Standing in front of Emmanuel's, I catch sight of my reflection in the window, I feel like Scrooge with the ghost of Christmas past. The clothes are all out of season now and the vacuum's been abandoned in the middle of the shop floor. I guess whoever locked up thought they'd sort it out the next morning, but that morning never came. In fact, come to think of it, it was probably me, but it feels so long ago now, I can't actually remember. I peer in to see what else has been left and notice a mannequin half-dressed right at the back of the store. A chill sneaks down the back of my neck, making me shudder again. The town has a really solemn, sad and hostile feel to it and I don't feel welcome.

I tear myself away from Emmanuel's, taking the back paths down towards the beach to meet Beau, I'll be a bit early but I can sit and bask in the sun before he turns up. I'm quite enjoying myself, strolling through the cobbled streets, admiring all the pretty houses, cottages and gardens. Some of these cottages must be over three hundred years old and it must cost a bomb to keep up the thatched roofs. You'd surely have to be a millionaire to be able to afford to live in one of those. One cottage catches my eye, it has a powder pink picket fence and a beautiful children's playhouse in the huge front garden. What a lucky kid to have that, it looks handmade. The wooden tree house has a slide and a rope tyre swing attached to it and it's painted in all the colours of the rainbow. I'd love to climb inside and see how it has been decked out, I bet it has carpet and not cheap carpet either. There's also a red chair hammock hanging from an enormous apple tree, the hammock is facing the treehouse, I expect so the mum can keep one eye on her kids whilst she relaxes and reads a book.

I'm so busy nosing at this person's house that at first, I don't see Cheska and Jake standing at the corner outside the little Co-op. It's her I spot first but I have to do a double take as she looks different. Her hair is down and sleek and past her shoulders. Instead of wearing a mask and the screwed up angry face she had when we bickered in the egg aisle, she's smiling and actually looks really pretty. Jake's smiling too, he's smiling at the little boy and chatting to him. I know Flynn said they worked together so I guess they bumped into each other, but what would he be doing over here?

I swiftly seek cover behind an old phone box to get a closer look. The little boy runs off and sits on the grass to play with his new toy and eat his sweets, out of earshot of Cheska and Jake. It's then that both their expressions change. She seems to be lecturing him about something, he replies, with a pleading, begging face but I'm not close enough to hear what they're saying. I wonder if she's lecturing him about me and our encounter in the supermarket? A man walks past with his dog and it barks loudly, bounding towards me with its mouth open, drawing attention. It's fight or flight. Confront or clear off. My body decides for me before any thoughts can enter my head, legs sprinting off in the opposite direction. I turn down the nearest side street to hide from them, praying that they didn't see me. Running as fast as I can, my legs burn as I run all the way to the beach to meet Beau.

Something stinks.

And it's not Jake's beard anymore.

Chapter Twelve

11 weeks into Lockdown – 8th June 2020

I didn't think I'd be here eleven weeks into lockdown but the pandemic has forced people into strange situations.

You find yourself doing things you wouldn't imagine doing. Today, I'm meeting up with Daniel and Lisa in Daniel's garden. This is the first time I've seen them out of a work setting and I probably wouldn't ever have seen them socially if it wasn't for the virus. Daniel has news about work. He has a mate in HR who's been filling him in on all the latest news and, in his words, he says he has the ultimate belter piece of scandal on Zeze, so how could I say no to that? None of us three kept our jobs at Emmanuel's, so now we're facing redundancy which I'm both scared and secretly pleased about. It felt good to drive out of town, to get away from it all and everyone who knows me. The music was on full blast in the car and the windows were down. I felt young and carefree again, it's been a while since I've felt like that.

♥ ♥ ♥

I smooth down my dress, a 1930's style tea dress, dusky pink with blue and purple butterflies all over it. I stayed up all night finishing it, wanting to look my best, but this morning I had such big bags under my eyes that I've had to use half a bottle of concealer to hide them. It's aged me by ten years so today my sunglasses will remain glued to my face in case Daniel recoils at my badger eyes. Thank God it's sunny.

Daniel lets me in through the back gate and I sigh when I see his garden. It's beautiful. The grass is freshly mown and towards the back of the garden, a wicker table and four wicker chairs with black and red checked cushions sit on the sun-bleached decking. Giant daisies, poppies and sunflowers are dotted around the edge of the garden. It's so neat and tidy. So quaint. There's a small wooden shed at the end of the garden, it's been painted light blue and looks like a mini beach hut. There's an identical mini blue wooden shed next to it, I assume this is for his beloved cat with the human name, Dave. It makes me smile. Daniel makes me smile.

'Everything *alight?*' Daniel asks in his Manchester drawl, his eyes boring into mine as if he knows what I'm thinking. I'm pretty sure he can only see his reflection in my mirror lenses but nevertheless. His aftershave smells delicious, just faint but it makes me feel all fluttery and lightheaded. Don't do anything stupid, Alannah. Just friends. You are still with Jake even if he is acting like a complete arsehole. And, anyway, I couldn't even if I wanted to as its still two metres social distancing. How long will this go on for? In March, I thought it would be completely over by the beginning of May at the very latest, but now it's June.

No touching.

This makes him all the more alluring of course.

Dammit.

'Yes, I'm fine, just a bit hot from the drive. You have a gorgeous garden. Lisa not here yet?' My intention is to sound cool like him, but for some reason I'm speaking incredibly fast, resembling Alvin from the chipmunks. Fail.

'Not yet. It's good to see you. I'll just go and grab the drinks, what do you fancy?' He tilts his head to the side and bites his lip, it's as if he can read my mind.

You. I want you.

'A coke or something will be fine, thanks.' I flash him a smile, plonk my bags down by the table and sit down on one of the wicker chairs. He swaggers off inside the house and I notice his garden backs out onto a lot of other gardens. I wonder if they all spy on each other having BBQs or sunbathing. It feels a bit intrusive; my eyes wander up to the house adjacent, I can see directly into their bathroom, glass shower screen and all.

Daniel strides back into the garden, his shirt, similar in pattern to the wicker chair cushions is undone, revealing a spattering of ginger chest hair. Well, I wasn't expecting that. I wonder what else is ginger? Do the curtains match the carpet?

'Here you go,' he says cheerfully as he places two glasses of coke down on the table. I take out my hand sanitiser and wipe my hands and around the glass before reaching into my bag for a straw.

'Sorry, got to be safe.' I shrug my shoulders, feeling ridiculous at the awkwardness and absurdity of it all. Daniel looks as if he is about to say something when we both jump at the loud banging noise coming from the back gate. There's a dog barking along with the banging, the dog, sounding angrier at every knock. I gulp down a mouthful of coke, the barking's putting me on edge.

'Hi guys, it's me, stop snogging and let me in,' Lisa shouts through the fence, giggling to herself. I blush, hoping my makeup hides my beetroot face. Daniel looks at me, smiles a big wide smile, then rolls his eyes and strides over to the gate to let her in. Lisa bowls into the garden with her dog who's bouncing around like a mad thing beside her.

'Sit down, Bryan. SIT.' The dog goes round sniffing everyone and everything before finally sitting down. Lisa gets a water bottle out and starts squirting water into its mouth as the dog guzzles it down like a baby goat, feeding from its mother.

'Cute dog, Lis, what breed is he again?' I ask, feigning interest, I'm not massively keen on dogs. I got bitten by one when I was a child. It was a poodle of all things, not the type of dog you would imagine to be violent. All the kids were playing down the cul-de-sac and a neighbour had a friend over who just let their dog run wild in the street. The kids were playing fetch with it happily until it made a beeline for me and bit me on the leg. Eight stitches later and Mum was fuming, she said you should never trust animals. They are unpredictable, sometimes worse than humans. I was only seven but I remember that comment sticking with me.

'Bryan's a Jug,' Lisa announces proudly.

'A what?' Daniel laughs and spits out his drink.

'A Jug, you know, a mix between a Jack Russel and a pug,' Lisa replies, pointing at her dog like we're both idiots.

'Oh yeah that famous breed, the Jug. What is it with all these fancy crossbreeds now? I'm going to sound like an old man when I say this but when I was a lad, they were just called mongrels.'

Lisa puts her hands over her dog's ears and gasps dramatically.

'You can't call dogs mongrels anymore. That's so insulting. And yes, you do sound ancient, very old fashioned for a man in his early thirties. What's next? Should *children* be seen and not heard?'

Daniel and I look at each other, not sure whether to laugh or not. Luckily, Lisa bursts out laughing at us.

'It's political correctness gone mad I know, but I love that he's a Jug. And it could be worse, imagine the name merge of a Shih Tzu and a poodle.' She laughs then pulls Bryan close to her by the collar and starts speaking in a baby voice and kissing him on his little yappy dog mouth. 'My little juggy wuggy Bryan, yes you are, yes you are my baby boy, yes you are,' she coos.

I look away feeling uncomfortable and catch Daniel's eye again, he grins then waggles a finger around by his temple insinuating Lisa's gone crazy. I press my lips together and try not to laugh. Bryan is Lisa's lockdown baby. She got him to keep her and the kids from killing each other, she said it's given everyone purpose, something to focus on.

'Okaaaay,' Daniel says slowly, giving me a side eye. 'Lisa, drink?' he asks, already getting up to go back into the house.

'Oooh yes please, got anything alcoholic? Him indoors is picking me up.' She winks, referring to her husband.

'Sure, beer or wine?' Daniel asks, standing with his legs far apart and hands behind his back, he looks like he's about to sing, I wonder if that's his stance on stage, very Liam Gallagher. I'm sure he said he does gigs.

'Wine all the time, my darling,' she says, still looking at Bryan lovingly.

'This is the perfect weather for a glass of wine, isn't it? So annoying I'm driving,' I pipe up, then blush with the worry that I sound desperate, an alcoholic or both.

'You can have wine.' Daniel cocks his head and moves his sun glasses down to look at me. 'Just stay over,' he continues casually.

I can't work out if he's joking or not.

'Wow, did you hear that? If that isn't an invitation then I don't know what is. Where's she going to sleep though?' Lisa sings and I give her the death stare. Why is she so hell bent on encouraging me to have an affair? The flowers could have really got me in trouble but Jake still thinks they're from Lisa. My thoughts turn to Jake at home alone and a pang of guilt hits me. I should talk to him; I should ask him what the hell is going on but part of me is afraid of what he might say and the other part is angry with him for being a dick.

'I'm sorry, I can't, it's not allowed anyway is it? Maybe another time,' I reply primly, whilst still managing to sound like a hussy. I've basically said, I won't do it now but keep trying and I might. God, I make myself die at times. Daniel goes off into the house and I glare at Lisa until he's gone inside.

'What?' Lisa screeches, holding her hands up.

'Just stop it,' I hiss. 'You're going to get me into trouble. The flowers, the remarks. Please stop. He's hot yes, anyone can see that but I'm also in a relationship and have been for quite some time.' I fold my arms in annoyance and to emphasise my point. Lisa looks wounded and we both sit in an awkward silence until she finally speaks.

'Sorry, Alannah. It's just you're still so young and

from what you've told me about Jake, I think you could be missing a chance here. I certainly missed mine.' She looks off into the distance and the penny drops. This isn't about me.

'Care to share?' I say gently.

Lisa sighs heavily, her expression turning wistful.

'It was nothing, just someone I met, but we were both married. We couldn't. He wouldn't, he already had kids. It was fifteen years ago now but I think of him every day. Still.' She sniffs and one big fat tear rolls slowly down her cheek.

'Oh Lis,' I say quietly as Daniel approaches with her wine. She wipes away her tear quickly with the back of her hand, her expression switching from sad to chirpy in milliseconds. She gulps down almost half the glass of wine then points at my bags, excitedly tapping her feet on the floor.

'Is that what I think it is?' she squeals.

'Oh yes! How could I forget?' How could I forget indeed? I've been working my arse off on this dress for weeks. 'Keep the bag, I hope you like it and I hope it fits,' I say nervously, clasping my hands together in prayer. Lisa goes into her handbag and retrieves hand sanitiser and a big block of sanitiser wipes, she does her hands first with the sanitiser, then a thorough wipe of the bag, dress and matching face mask. It suddenly makes me feel very dirty. I know that's silly as this is just procedure now but I can't help think how weird it looks and she also didn't wipe the wine glass, or the chair come to think of it, so really, what's the point?

'Oh Alannah, you absolute genius,' she screams, examining the dress and matching face mask. 'They are stunning. Just stunning.' She stands up and holds her dress up against her, swaying from side to side watching the fabric swish. Then without any warning, whips off the dress she's already wearing and pulls on the new dress. Poor Daniel chokes on his drink.

'Looks nice Lis, but can't say the same about your granny pants.' Daniel sniggers before sticking his fingers down his throat, pretending to be sick. Lisa, is completely unphased.

'Oh piss off you, when a woman gets to a certain age, it's all she wears so get used to it my love,' she replies, admiring herself in her dress and face mask, taking photos with her phone as she twirls around in the garden. Bryan, meanwhile is barking and snapping at the hem of the dress. I scowl inwardly at the dog; I hope the little jug ferret doesn't rip it.

'Is that so? And do you wear granny pants yet, Alannah? I bet you don't, you look like a French knickers kinda gal.' Daniel looks me up and down intensely. I might as well be sat here naked as I feel totally transparent now. Can he tell? Can he see my underwear through my dress? Is the fabric too thin?

'Oh no, I'm not quite there yet.' I lie, cringing because that is exactly what I'm wearing. I've always gone for comfort over looks regarding my underwear. Jake has never been that fussed either, he prefers nothing at all so why spend loads of money on uncomfortable, cheese grater knickers when no one will appreciate them. Going by Daniel's comment he is definitely into his women wearing nice lingerie.

'Now then, ladies.' Daniel claps his hands together, changing the conversation as I'm clearly squirming in my seat. In my massive, secret, comfy, granny knickers. 'You want to hear the latest news from Emmanuel's?' he says in a low, sinister voice that I find incredibly sexy.

'Yes please,' Lisa and I chirp in unison.

'Okay, well my secret HR source has informed me that Cherry got the job for our region so she'll be managing the southwest store.' He leans back in his seat, crossing his arms behind his head.

'Oh, what a surprise,' I say rolling my eyes, picturing Cherry's pleased cat bum smug mouth. It's always the arse lick.

'I'm not surprised either, she was Zeze's little pet pooch,' Lisa adds, giving Bryan a kiss on the mouth.

'Is that it?' I ask.

Good luck to Cherry. We still haven't been told if we're going or not, the email from HR says we are being considered for redundancy. There has to be a consultation first, so that's a Zoom call with Manni next week to drag it out a little longer. We haven't had our scores back for our work performance either. I don't see the point; we know we're going and the reasons people have been picked are definitely not based on the scores. There's only a limited number of spaces but I guess there's procedures to follow. Don't bother.

'No, no, there's more, that's just the taster ladies,' Daniel says slowly, enjoying the power of his knowledge.

'Oooh tantalising.' Lisa flirts, wriggling her shoulders.

'Well, she's gone. Zeze has gone.' He waits for our reaction and we both blink at him. 'Rachael got the area manager's job. They'll be an email out from HR soon announcing it along with who the managers are.'

'But she lives in Scotland, doesn't she?' I say, frowning.

'I know, so stupid, but I guess she won't visit much

and will just do a lot of it on the phone and by email.' Daniel raises his eyebrows then folds his arms behind his head, displaying his golden chest hair.

'I'm surprised Zeze didn't get it, Manni loves her.'

'Well you'd be right there, Lisa. Zeze was set on getting the area manager's role, she'd obviously rigged it so that favourite Cherry would get the manager's job down in the Southwest and they could work together. Cherry does anything and everything Zeze asks.'

'Arse lick' I interject and Lisa sniggers.

'She marked you down on the questionnaire a right treat, Alannah,' Daniel continues. 'She only gave you a one for attitude. Hmmm I wonder what you did to piss her off?' Daniel smirks, tilting his head to the side playfully.

'The cheek. Probably right though because I did puke all over her designer suit.'

Lisa snorts and Daniel laughs, holding his stomach. I told them both about it a few weeks ago on WhatsApp and was then inundated with puking memes from Lisa for two days. Daniel composes himself and carries on.

'She'd had several meetings with Manni, pushing her business plan. It was looking promising for her to get the area manger role. Manni's always liked her, she talks a good talk.'

'And then what?' Lisa squawks, sounding as impatient as I feel.

'Well, you're never gonna believe this,' Daniel teases.

'Oh my God, say it,' I screech.

'Lance complained about her a while ago, on the day of the infamous Zoom call, about a number of different occasions. They were quite serious complaints too and weren't taken lightly by HR.'

'Lance?' Lisa and I shriek in puzzled unison at him.

'Yup. Sexual harassment,' Daniel delivers the news then pauses as Lisa and I gasp. 'Apparently, she used to come into his shop and have a right old grope of his arse when there was no one about, it got worse just before we got locked down as there were hardly any staff or customers. Once, she tried stroking his bits in the stock room, pretending she was reaching for a jumper or something. The straw that broke the camel's back was that Zoom call. She should have taken the responsibility as area manager to abort the call as soon as he came on screen with his gonads out but she watched until the end, pervy old Zeze.'

'Oh yuk. Poor Lance,' I say, feeling guilty again for also participating in the Zoom call until the bitter end. Zeze didn't strike me as the type but she *was* always quite tactile with young male customers come to think of it, then there's that time Jake picked me up after I was sick, she was weird then. Zeze the Sleazy.

'Is he seriously traumatised by it?' Lisa asks, looking concerned.

'I wouldn't say traumatised, he always used to laugh it off and got away with a lot because she liked him but after the Zoom call, he confided in his girlfriend about everything and she went ape shit. It was her that encouraged him to file a complaint. It's taken a long time and a lot of interviews with Lance and Zeze separately on Zoom. Of course, she denied it all so it was his word against hers, there was nothing they could do apart from just choose another area manager and make her redundant.'

'Well, they made them both redundant didn't they so Zeze's got away with it and Lance has in effect been punished for speaking up,' Lisa comments then glugs down the rest of her wine before reaching into her handbag for a miniature bottle of apple flavoured vodka and a packet of snacking ham.

Daniel nods then carries on. 'They even dug into her past jobs again and they're waiting to hear back on several character references. I'll keep you ladies updated on that.'

'What, can they even do that?'

'Well, they are, Alannah. I don't know what they hope to achieve as she's gone now anyway but I reckon there's more to it,' Daniel replies.

'Yeah, I guess he may want to take her to court and if she's been reported before, then that may help his case. Shit,' Lisa adds before taking another swig from her vodka bottle.

'It's just revolting. It's sick. How could she do that? In a way it's so much worse because you would never expect that of her. Dirty old woman. Sleazy Zeze should be punished for this, she could go on to do it again and next time it could be so much worse. She disgusts me.' I'm on a rant.

We spend the next couple of hours discussing work and Zeze the Sleazy until Lisa gets horribly drunk on her miniature vodka bottle stash and starts hiccupping, suggesting Daniel and I run away together and embark on a wild romance. She then starts crying about her lost love and we spend an hour calming her down before 'him indoors' comes to collect her.

I take that as my cue to leave.

On the drive home, I can't stop thinking about Zeze and poor Lance.

I knew there was something off about Zeze from the moment I met her but I never expected it to be that. Never in a million years. I guess you never know what's going on in someone else's mind. People are unpredictable, just like that poodle.

Chapter Thirteen

Daniel: *It was really nice seeing you yesterday. Lisa is a character, isn't she? That bloody Jug though.*

Me: *It was great to see you guys too. Still can't believe all that about Zeze. I can't stop thinking about it. Yes, she certainly is that. The Jug was cute in a strange way but also very yappy and licky. I think I left with a cup full of its saliva on my feet.*

I shudder at the thought of it. In the end I had to pinch one of Lisa's industrial sanitiser wipes to wash my feet down from all of Bryan's spit. Yuk.

Daniel: *You're funny, you really make me smile a lot. This may be a bit full on but I can't stop thinking about you. Sorry if that's too much but life is too short to not say how you feel.*

My stomach drops. I turn my phone off in a panic, sit on the sofa and stare into the blank TV screen. Oh God, how do I reply to that? What have I encouraged? I'll leave it for now. The truth is, I do find him attractive, anyone would but there's no way I can say that to Daniel.

Jake.

I need to speak to Jake and work out what the hell is going on with us, I've been putting it off for way too long. I don't want to just throw it all away over a silly crush and petty arguments. He isn't home, hasn't been all day. I heard him get up at the crack of dawn, he came into the bedroom to get some clothes and get changed and off he went. Again.

I do the only other thing there is to do at the moment and go for a walk. It's still early evening, warm and sunny, the fresh air will do me good. The beach beckons. I grab my things, leaving my phone at home because I don't want to engage with technology right now. As I get nearer to the beach, there are loads of cars parked all along the road and someone is trying to parallel park into a space that they definitely aren't going to fit into.

Tourists.

I watch a family of four squeeze their camping chairs, other beach paraphernalia and kids into the boot and back seats of their car before speeding off down the road. The woman attempting to parallel park, clocks them leaving and nips into their space just in time. She gets out of the car and her dog jumps out behind her, jumping up and down with pent up energy. We say hello and I vaguely recognise her; she tells me it was much busier earlier and she had to go back home as the whole road was packed. The fact that she's said hello and had a conversation with me makes me think she must be a local, most tourists tend to ignore everyone around them, in their own little tourist bubble.

Before lockdown happened, a lot come from London to escape city life and now the rules have been relaxed, they have returned tenfold. When I've visited London, on the handful of occasions that I've been, I always felt completely out of place. No one says hello, it's incredibly busy and quite unfriendly, people just don't have time to stop and say hi. I've spent my whole life in Coolsbay, it's beautiful, why would I want to be anywhere else? *Perhaps for work if you can't get anything here, beggars can't be choosers*, a little inner voice torments me. My heart thuds in my chest.

Before Emmanuel's, I worked in a smaller clothes shop on the other end of the high street and previous to that I worked at The Coolsbay Hotel on reception, which I hated. My boss was nasty with a just as nasty puffy combover that he used to tease across his head every day. One day he trimmed it for whatever reason and it never reached the other side of his head ever again. It gave it a lot more volume but left a little tramline running down the side of his scalp pointing directly to his ear hair. After that, we called him Road Runner.

The customers loved to complain incessantly at that hotel, we seemed to get a lot of people working away, especially when the cruise ships came in. All sorts of important people would turn up, making demands. I sigh at the thought of it. Three jobs and I'm thirty-two, I guess when you think about it that isn't a lot. The whole idea of having to job hunt is very depressing, there's absolutely no one local recruiting, apart from the supermarket and I don't think I'd be very good there, anyway they might recognise me after my showdown with Cheska, and turn me straight down. I can hear the manager's response already. *'Sorry we don't employ people who verbally abuse fellow customers, it's a policy of ours that we take very seriously.'*

The sight of the beach pulls me out of self-pity mode instantly. It's an absolute shit hole of the worst kind. So awful that I let out an almighty groan, causing people to look at me accusingly. On a very busy day, there's always a bit of rubbish but this is a whole new level. There's no sign of sand, just a beach full of rubbish. I trail through it all until I get to the little cove, not many tourists know about it but I can see that people have been here too as it's also covered in rubbish. Apart from a couple sitting up against some rocks and someone who's bent down attempting to clean up the rubbish, there's no one else at the cove anymore. I desperately scout around, searching for somewhere to sit, rubbish free, for five minutes. It's no good, I start to trudge off back through the sea of crap and head for home. This is just infuriating.

'Alannah,' says a muffled voice from behind a facemask. 'It's me.'

I squint at the huge black facemask, dark hair tied up and tanned muscled arms, unable to recognise him until he gets closer. It's Flynn.

'Hey, I almost didn't recognise you with all that gear, I think it was the hi-vis that threw me,' I reply, pushing my hair behind my ears.

'Oh yes, I like to look professional.' He takes off his hi-vis and face mask then stuffs them into his bag.

'Your hair too, looks different,' I say more to myself than to him, the top of his hair is scooped up in a man bun. He resembles Keanu Reeves crossed with that guy out of game of thrones, Kit, I think his name is. Not a bad combo if you like that kind of thing.

'Oh yeah, this isn't my new look.' Flynn wipes his forehead and grimaces. 'It just gets in the way of my eyes when picking all of this up.' He holds his arms out to highlight all the shit on the beach and I nod sadly.

'How can people do this?' I agree loudly. The couple

sat against the rocks start to make a quick, guilty getaway as Flynn and I glance over in their direction. They take their rubbish, every crumb, and leave. Good.

'Why don't you help?' I have loads of rubbish bags and some spare gloves. No facemasks though, so if you want to wear one, you'd have to wear your own.'

'Yeah, I'd like that, I've got a mask somewhere in here.' I rummage in my bag and put on one of my homemade facemasks, giving him the thumbs up. 'So how come you're doing this? Is it a side business? Or are you working for the council now?' I mumble through my facemask to him, feeling like a complete prat. Why did I put the facemask on now, why not finish the conversation with him first and then put it on? Suddenly I'm very conscious that this particular facemask is very tight behind my ears which forces them to poke forward a lot. When I breathe the fabric sucks in and out making me sound like Darth Vader. I try to breathe quieter.

'Oh no, no, I'm not employed to do this. I'm just sick of it. I come here most days for an hour or so, helps to pass the time too.' He smiles shyly. He sounds lonely. I stop myself from asking how he is at this point as he puts on a fresh facemask and we can't have a two-way muffled conversation, especially with my uncomfortable facemask malfunction. But I will ask him, right after we've cleaned up our beloved cove and my ears can return to their normal position.

The rubbish we come across is unbelievable. A used sanitary towel being one of the vilest things I find, along with a couple of soiled nappies and copious amounts of cans, rotting/stale food and wrappers. It's satisfying to clear it all up though. Flynn and I make a nice little team and get the cove tidied up in no time.

He picks up the last bit of rubbish and we sit down on the now clean sand, two metres apart. We rip our facemasks off and I let out a little moan as my ears ping back. As I massage them back to their normal position, Flynn shows me his finds. We haven't been paid for this but actually, we've done pretty well. Flynn's found a twenty-pound note plus change and I've found about a tenner in change. All in all, not bad pay for under an hour's work. Small perks for clearing up other people's crap.

'I've also found this, but I think I'll have to hand it in to the police, or that would be proper stealing,' Flynn says, showing me a fancy smart phone. It looks expensive.

'Yep, we can't get away with that one, a few pounds are one thing, someone's phone is another. Although I'm tempted, we'd get a lot for that on eBay.' We both laugh as Flynn examines the phone, nodding in agreement.

'Hey, we could make a living out of this. Tidy up the beach and sell or keep anything decent that we find. Perfect,' I joke.

Flynn smiles and looks down at his feet, burying his toes into the sand.

'So, how's things with you at the moment?' I ask, changing the subject. 'Fitness classes and everything still going well?' The "everything" is Becky, of course. I haven't seen her on Flynn's balcony for weeks, and weeks. She could have it. The virus. That would explain everything. Perhaps they haven't told us because they don't want to frighten us.

Please don't let her have it.

'It's good. I mean the fitness stuff is going well. It's busy, a lot of people want to try and stay fit during all

125

this. It's so easy to become a couch potato when you can't go anywhere.' He stretches his muscular arms out in front of him before lifting them over his head to stretch his shoulders out. I think of Jake, the couch potato. He doesn't look like one any longer, not since he's been exercising and training again but whenever he is at home, he's slumped on that couch like the biggest couch potato going. Resentment bubbles inside me about him and the zombies.

'What about you? Is that one of your own creations again?' He points at my dress.

'It is, yes. I'm impressed you noticed.'

'Well, I am very observant.'

'That you are.'

'Yup.'

'How's Becky? I haven't seen her on the balcony in a while. Is she alright?' I hold my breath. Please can she be okay. I feel bad for not asking before.

'Yeah, she's fine,' he mumbles into his chest, drawing circles in the sand with his fingers.

'And, are you okay?' I ask, moving my hair out of my face and rubbing my ears which are still aching from the mask.

'I'm fine.' There's a tone to his voice that I haven't heard before. I can't quite place it. Sadness. Boredom. Resentment – perhaps that's it, I recognise it only too well.

'Really, are you sure?' I try again, hoping that I'm not pushing it. She could be led in a hospital bed for all I know, hooked up to a ventilator. Please no.

'Becky doesn't live with me anymore,' he blurts out, then searches my face for a response, his amber eyes glowing with emotion.

'Oh,' is all I manage then kick myself for not

offering sympathy straightaway.

'Indeed, oh. She got caught shagging her colleague in the gym car park. A few months ago, now.'

My hand flies up to my mouth and it's now I wish I still had the painful facemask on. Perfect Becky was bonking someone else. The shock of it makes me giggle nervously, not at Flynn's situation but at Becky big bum bonking in the car park. How skanky. He offers a glimmer of a smirk then the words come tumbling out, as if they've been trapped inside him for too long.

'The security cameras picked it up. They would meet there in the middle of the day in their separate cars and then Becky would get in his car for a good seeing to. What they didn't know was that it was all over CCTV and the security guards were still working.'

'Why?' Why would anyone do that to Flynn?

'The security guards keep an eye on the lake that surrounds the gym as it has expensive fish in it, people have tried to steal them in the past. They thought it would get worse during lockdown.' His fingers swirl more quickly in the sand making a figure of eight as the story falls out. He stops for a second and I'm sure I see them trembling. Poor, sweet Flynn.

'I'm so sorry, Flynn.' I wish I could put my arm around him and tell him he was too good for her anyway. She was always so self-centred and vain. Becky big bum.

'No, don't be. I'm better off without her. It was more humiliating than anything else. The security guards told the facilities manager and her husband told me. An old mate from school, he even offered to show me the tapes. Of course, I declined. Couldn't watch that, so I confronted Becky. Her face said it all but she still tried to deny it.'

'Shit. Was it with anyone we know?'

'No, don't think so, just one of the other personal trainers that works there. A young lad, very young. Think he's about nineteen.' Flynn curls his lip in disgust.

'Wow. Well I didn't have her down as a cradle snatcher,' I say and Flynn sniggers, making faster circles with his fingers in the sand.

'Neither did I, and not only that, apparently, she was seen putting a lead on him.'

'A lead?'

'A dog lead. The best bit, he wore a facemask.' Flynn scoffs.

'To stop breathing in the germs? Not much point really is there if they're bumping uglies anyway.' Woops perhaps shouldn't have said that.

'Yes and no. I don't know. It had a picture of a dog's mouth and nose on it. Looked like an Alsatian apparently.' Flynn shakes his head then laughs lightly, still in disbelief.

'Wow, that takes dogging to a whole new level. Christ on a bike,' I blurt out, sounding more like my brother than ever. We both make a face at each other, at the image now etched into our minds. Flynn must have been carrying that image around with him all on his own for months. Bless him.

'Why didn't you say anything before? At the beach, on my birthday? I was drivelling on about Jake and you didn't mention Becky?' This must have happened way before my birthday. I think of all the quizzes she's been absent from and try to remember when I last saw her. Perhaps the last time was when Jake and I had our date night and he asked to borrow money.

'Dunno, I was ashamed. It's kind of embarrassing

that she would choose a teenage pup over me.'

'I guess.' I bite my lip, supressing a giggle but one escapes.

'See, it's laughable.' Flynn groans. He rubs his eyes with his hands, then laughs, despite himself.

'You're right. You are better off without her but I wish you'd said something and not suffered in silence. Does Jake know?'

'No, just you. I haven't told anyone else.'

I grip the sand in between my fingers.

'Well, we aren't exactly speaking at the moment, me and Jake,' I open up. Now it's me making swirls in the sand. Big fat circles, getting deeper and deeper.

After a big awkward pause Flynn asks, 'How come?'

After a deep breath, I tell him everything, filling in the gaps from my birthday. About how Jake's been avoiding me. The stupid constant arguments over nothing. The moods, lending his mum money and finally the meeting I saw between him and Cheska.

'Nothing's going on between those two is it?' I blush, self-conscious for asking. Feeling silly at the assumption.

'Not that I know of. I mean no, of course not.' Flynn shakes his head but is he trying to convince himself as much as me?

'It's just that when I saw them, it was weird, like they were disagreeing over something. Why would they be arguing?'

'No idea.' Flynn frowns and runs his fingers over his jaw.

'How well do they know each other? It's just he's never mentioned her before,' I probe, feeling like a trainee detective.

'We all used to work together, about twelve years

ago now. We were young, we'd all go on nights out and get smashed. They may have kissed a few times but that's as far as it went.'

'Right.'

Chapter Fourteen

I sprint home from the beach, faster than I've ever run before. It's super muggy now and salty sweat seeps through my body as I taste the sticky bitterness.

I'm going to have it out with Jake. Once and for all.

As my flipflops slap the pavement, my mind works overtime with thoughts of him and Cheska. Then there's Daniel. I still haven't replied. When this is all over, I'll message him back, although I have no idea what I'll say.

I finally get to my front door and rummage in my bag for my keys. My hand touches a crumpled-up bit of paper and I pick it out to see what it is. It's Bet's shopping list. I kick myself. Shit. I was meant to go shopping for her. I've also made her a dress that I was going to surprise her with. It's a thank you for helping and inspiring me with my sewing. I hadn't told her I was making it, partly because I wanted it to be a surprise but also because she'd refuse and say not to bother. I can't let her down, God knows how long I'll be with Jake and she could be sitting there without any food or milk to have with her tea. She relies on me; looks forward to my visits. I've waited weeks to confront Jake so what's another thirty minutes or so.

I run back down the stairs and hop in my car, the shopping only takes me twenty minutes and I make sure to buy myself a bottle of wine, I'll be needing this after my confrontation with Jake. I park the car, run back up the stairs and nip in my flat to get the dress. I'm outside Bet's flat for 6pm, the time we agreed. Setting the shopping down, I bang on the door and I'm even more sweaty and out of breath than before.

I wait but there's no answer. Unusual.

Bang. Bang. Bang. I try again.

Still no answer. I peer through the letter box and shout through into the living room. Surely, she will hear me now.

'Bet, it's Alannah. I've got your shopping and a little surprise,' I sing. Still no answer.

'Bet, are you there?' I raise my voice, desperately trying to keep the stiff letter box open to prevent it from snapping down on my fingers. 'Bet?' I don't have a spare key. 'Bet, are you okay? Are you hurt?' My calls are met with an empty silence.

Nothing.

I reach into my handbag for my phone and call Beau, he'll know what to do and he's close by. It rings and rings. No answer. I consider calling Flynn but he was staying at the beach to tidy up some more. Jake's inside the flat, he was slumped on the sofa when I got the dress.

'Jake, Bet won't answer the door, I'm worried,' I blurt out as I re-enter our flat.

He looks up reluctantly from his phone.

'Okay, she's probably asleep or something, she's old. They have naps,' he says, shrugging his shoulders before going back to his phone.

'No, it's not like her, we arranged a time.' I wipe the

sweat from my forehead with my hand and wipe it on the side of my clothes.

'I'm sure she's fine,' he says flatly.

'Jake, I think we need to try and get in, call the police or something.' I suddenly feel like I'm overreacting. She probably is fine. I'm sure she is fine. No, but what if she isn't?

'Doesn't matter,' I snap and leave the flat. If he's going to make this difficult then I'll get help elsewhere. I bang on Bet's door again and still nothing. She wasn't even going out for walks so there isn't anywhere else she could be apart from inside her flat. I'll ring Flynn and if he doesn't answer then I guess the next step will be to call the police. Flynn picks up almost immediately.

'Flynn, it's me. It's Bet. She isn't answering her door. I'm so worried, can you try and get in? Bang the door down or something.'

'Okay, don't worry, I'm almost at my flat now, I'll be five minutes.'

'Okay, thanks. Bye.'

'Alannah, you still there?'

'Yes, what's up?'

'Nothing. Just stay calm okay, I'll be there soon.'

'Yep.'

I hang up and continue to bang on Bet's door and her other neighbour's door until Flynn arrives. The neighbours answer and say they haven't seen her on the balcony for a few days and come to think of it, neither have I. She's usually out on the balcony every day come rain or shine seeing to her hanging baskets, she calls it her mini-sanctuary. They don't have a spare key. Bet's never given me a spare key either, never had a reason to.

'Flynn!' I call as he approaches, relieved to see him.

'You okay?' Flynn reaches into his pocket and retrieves a key. It's Bet's spare key. Thank God.

'Let me just go in for now.' Flynn forgets himself and touches my arm. His fingers leave an imprinted tingle of pins and needles. 'Stay here.' Tentatively, he opens the door and slowly walks into her flat as he calls Bet's name. Myself and Bet's neighbours, Pat and Jean, as well as my neighbours, Donna and Dominique who have now joined us, wait outside the door as instructed.

Flynn returns moments later.

'I've called an ambulance but I'm not sure. . .' he trails off, his voice shaky and his face pale.

'Did you find her?' Jean asks, arms folded, comforting herself. Pat and Jean are elderly, their little faces etched with worry.

'Is she okay, Flynn? What's happened?' I whimper. My eyes are already filled with tears as I search Flynn's face for answers.

'I've found her, I think she's had a fall,' Flynn says softly, his sad eyes say it all. Jean starts crying followed by Dominique, and their partners comfort them.

'Oh no. Please no,' I hear myself shriek like a wounded animal. My body bends over like I've been hit by a truck.

'Let me see her,' I sob, tears streaming down my face. 'I've got her shopping. I've made her a dress.'

'No, you shouldn't, you mustn't.' Flynn shakes his head. I try to get past him. 'No. You can't. Stop,' he says firmly, blocking off the entrance with his arm. I back off and he stares at me intensely with sombre, glassy eyes. 'We need to keep safe. You don't know what led to the fall. We can't risk it. The ambulance is on its way,' he says in a low voice, not letting go of my gaze.

♥ ♥ ♥

Bet was pronounced dead at the scene. The paramedics said it was likely she had passed away several hours before, but we won't know for sure until the post mortem. She'd fallen and banged her head on the kitchen worktop, which is what killed her. Jake came out minutes before the ambulance arrived, he must have heard all of the commotion. Flynn was comforting me as I balled into his shoulder and Jake pulled him off me, chastising him about social distancing and germs. Jake said he would deal with me, whatever that meant.

I still can't believe it. I must have been the last person to see her. She was chirpy and chatty as usual. I'd asked her if she wanted to be part of our social bubble so we could chat in comfort rather than standing at the door. She was over the moon. 'Are you sure you don't want your mum or one of your relatives dear?' she had asked. I told her that Mum had Gary and Beau can look after himself and that I would love Bet to be in my social bubble, but it never happened and now it never will. She smiled sweetly at me and told me that she was so grateful for everything, I'd been her lifeline during this crisis.

I can't stop thinking of her all alone. Did she suffer for long? Did she know she was going to die? Was she scared? I hope it was quick and painless. The paramedics were asking who her next of kin was. I think it's one of her children, the one that lives in the UK, up north, I had explained. But actually, I'm not completely sure. I feel so helpless, I didn't even have a spare key, I had to wait for Flynn. I've searched for her family on Facebook and found one of her children, but he lives in Australia, it's not like they can jump on a plane and fly over at the moment. After agonising over it for ages I ended up ringing the hospital and they advised that the family had already been contacted. They know she's gone.

The week crawls by and I pass the time sewing and crying. Jake comforts me but it's almost robotic and I haven't the emotional energy to discuss what I saw with him and Cheska. I stay up late into the night every night, doing as much as I can to keep busy. Sewing reminds me of Bet and it gives me a strange comfort to pass the time this way. It's also the only thing that makes me tired enough to sleep. Even the last dress I made was for Bet, I can't bring myself to make any more dresses right now so it's scrubs, masses of scrubs for the Coolsbay Scrub Hub. At least they're happy. Bet's food is in my fridge and her dress is still in its bag in my bedroom. I can't stop thinking about her and her family. I've been stalking her son on Facebook again, and eventually pluck up the courage to send him a message.

> Me: *Hello Michael, I'm Alannah and I was your mum's neighbour. I just wanted to reach out and say what a lovely lady she was and that I am so very sorry for your devastating loss. If there is anything I can do to help then please don't hesitate to ask. I know it's extra difficult at the moment with everything that's going on. Thinking of you and your family at this very sad time. Take care.*

He might not even reply but at least he'll know I'm here if Bet's family need me and if they need us to get into the flat then we can as Flynn has a key. I should have known he would have a key; he was always doing little favours for her before lockdown. He told me the last time he used it was when he'd let in some carpet fitters when Bet had to go on a last-minute visit up north to see her other son. She'd told Flynn she wanted a strong man there to keep them in check and make sure they were doing the job right. I wonder why she didn't ask Jake? Says a lot really. I check the time and work out that with a nine-hour difference it must be three in the morning in Australia so he isn't likely to see my message for a while. I scroll mindlessly through my phone and browse my Instagram account. I have a new message.

> Fashion blogger: *I would absolutely love to wear one of your dresses. You may think this a little cheeky but could I ask you to make three dresses? In a nautical theme, but each one different and with matching facemasks of course. I think once our followers see them on us, they will love it and be desperate to know where they can get one too. Let me know when you think you will have the dress ready by, I'll send our measurements over shortly if you're interested. I hope you're interested; we're really looking forward to working with you.*

Well, she doesn't want much. I sigh to myself. Demands for more dresses, face masks and a theme. She's more than a bit cheeky. I think back to all the dresses I've made for friends over the last few months, at least I've had practice. The fashion blogger has included the other two influencers in her message and I click on their profiles to have a nose. One of them has 1.8 million followers. I recognise her, she was on a reality TV show about finding love, Jake and I watched it at the start of lockdown. She wasn't lucky in love but she came across well and has clearly done very well for herself. Should I do it? I don't know, but Bet's voice echoes in my head with one of her many pearls of wisdom. *The most difficult thing is the decision to act, the rest is just tenacity.*' She's right I need to just get on with it and give it my all. After all, I have nothing to lose.

I'll do it for Bet.

Chapter Fifteen

3 months and 1 week into lockdown – will it ever end?

Beau looks at me like I've gone bat shit crazy.

'You need to talk to him, like I said. For God's sake, woman, what's wrong with you? Hasn't Bet dying taught you anything? Life's too short to waste time.' He bounces around re-positioning himself on my sofa until he finally gets comfortable and hoists one long leg up over the knee of the other. His leg catches the coffee table and it wobbles like my nerves. Beau's in our social bubble now, he is the only other person allowed in the flat at the moment. I asked Jake if that was alright and he just grunted so I took that as a yes.

'Careful, you nearly knocked my drink over, gangly,' I warn. 'And yes, I know. I'm concentrating on the dresses at the moment and I'm shattered. Anyway, I've tried. He gives me nothing,' I complain, sounding pathetic. Beau's right, what is wrong with me? We don't even get a chance to pick my behaviour to pieces as our conversation's cut short by Jake coming home. He strides into the living room, looking like Mr Grumpy as per usual.

'Hey, big man, what's cracking?' Beau taunts, with a smirk on his face.

'All good thank you,' Jake answers back, not looking at him, sounding completely disinterested. He pads into the kitchen, shoves a protein chocolate bar down his neck and begins making himself a protein shake.

'That's nice mate, aren't you going to ask me how I am? Or even better, ask how my sister is? You know the one you live with. Your girlfriend,' Beau annunciates the word girlfriend which makes me wince. He sits back and folds his arms behind his head, pleased with himself and the potential drama that he envisions unfolding. My eyes dart to Jake. I can't see his face but his back tenses through his yellow vest. This could get ugly.

'I see her every day mate, she's fine. Anyway, I'm off again. I have another client in a bit,' Jake replies but talks to his protein shake, then strides straight past us, as quickly as he can. But not before Beau lowers down one big gangly leg into his path.

'Ouch,' Jake yelps. 'Prick,' he mutters under his breath, stumbling over Beau's foot, spilling his protein shake in the process. He steadies himself and stands over my brother. Beau laughs, throwing his head back. He's enjoying this way too much.

'I'll be back in a couple of hours. Get him out of my flat by the time I get back,' he spits as he glares at Beau, his face beetroot red with rage.

'Maybe I will, maybe I won't,' I sing, sounding as childish as Beau is acting. It must run in the family. Jake doesn't look at me the entire time but instead just glares at Beau. It's as though he can't bear to look at me.

I disgust him.

'Pathetic, both of you.' Jake stomps off, slamming

the door behind him. I'm not sad anymore, I'm angry.

'I've had enough of this shit.' I stand up to my full height, feeling tall and powerful. There's a fire in my belly that won't be extinguished until I get to the bottom of this. 'Right, you start in the living room and kitchen, look through every drawer, leave no stone unturned.'

'Right, you weirdo, what am I looking for?' Beau stands up, rubbing his hands together, ready to support his sister's mission, whatever that might be.

'I don't know, anything, something. He won't communicate with me so we have to resort to other means.'

'Let's do this.' Beau punches the air.

'We haven't got long, put everything back at it was and shout me if you find anything.' I'm strangely excited. It's time.

'Roger.' Beau salutes me, then looks around helpless. I point to the coffee table drawer.

'Start there,' I instruct, and he salutes me again.

I march off to the bedroom and stand there overwhelmed for several seconds. I shouldn't be, the flat really isn't that big, it won't take long to have a good rifle through everything, why didn't I think of this before?

First, I flick through his side of the built-in wardrobe, combing through piles of crumpled up clothes that have been stuffed into the shelves. Checking pockets of jeans and trousers in anticipation of finding tell-tale receipts. Nothing. The chest of drawers gets a thorough checking too but I know I'm wasting my time as we share it, he wouldn't be stupid enough to hide anything in there, would he?

'Alannah. I think I've got something,' Beau shouts

and I pelt into the living room with my heart beating like a race horse. He's got a wooden box open with what looks like letters in it. I don't recognise it. He's holding one of the letters and waving it at me. I grab it out of his hand and read it. Hands trembling.

This could change everything.

Dear Jake,

These last few weeks have been like a whirlwind and I have loved every second of it. Your letter was so sweet, keep them coming. I've never felt this way before either and I can't wait until we can finally be together, properly. I hope you're enjoying the training; do you have any funny stories? Nothing to report here, just same old. Work is utterly boring at the moment. When you finish training, let's plan a holiday. Then let's plan the rest of our lives.

I love you so much

Take care

Your bear

xxx

Hot tears stream down my face. *Your bear.* The letters are from me, he kept them. That's what he used to call me, Alannah Bear. I totally forgot we used to write to each other. At the time he was training to be an electrician and had to go away on a three-week course about two months into our relationship. He did come home at weekends and stayed with me in my flat for most of it, popping home to see his mum in-between who was going through a break up, so he was there a fair bit too. We were both so smitten and decided to write to each other during the week when he was away. It was actually Jake's idea, we told each other how we felt pretty early on and writing to each other just felt so romantic, so new. I'd never had a love letter. The most I'd got before that was a Post-it Note in school from the class bully saying 'Ur fit.' Which was probably a joke as I definitely wasn't fit at school, face full of acne and the body of an overgrown stick insect, but I've grown into myself now. Jake didn't become an electrician; the course wasn't for him and that's when he came back early and started a new job at the gym and began training to become a personal trainer. A year later, we bought this flat together.

'Wow, this one's pretty graphic, bear is obviously a bit of a goer.' I look up to see Beau reading another letter and grab it out of his hand.

'Give me that. They aren't what you think,' I snap.

'No way man, I'm taking a photo of this, evidence.' Beau reaches for his phone and begins snapping away.

'No. Give it back. Stop. Delete that. They're from me,' I whine. Dying.

'Oh. Gross.' Beau drops the letter like he's just touched a shit. I feel a bit sorry for him, he knows way too much about his sister's bedroom antics now.

'Yeah.' I cringe. 'Listen I don't want to do this anymore, it's wrong. I'm going to speak to him when he gets back. No more searching.' I've got a headache now. The letters have reminded me how we used to feel about each other, how we used to be.

'If you're sure, sis? I mean, I bet we'll find something.' Beau raises an eyebrow then raises one side of his top lip as he looks at the letters.

'Yeah. I'm sure. It's just wrong.'

'Okay, I'll leave you to it then.' Beau looks at his watch. 'Shit, I really do have to go. I have to meet someone in twenty minutes.'

'Someone?' I enquire.

'Yeah, just a mate but I can't be late, we're going for a nature walk. Trying to reconnect with mother earth.'

'How romantic.' I snort. Beau is a walking oxymoron. Tripping up my boyfriend, acting like the class bully in one breath and then all nature, zen and yoga in the next.

'Maybe.' He shrugs nonchalantly. 'Alright, keep me posted, shout if you need me.' Beau heads towards my front door.

'Will do,' I reply, staring at the pretty pink stone he's just placed in my hand.

'Rose quartz. It's good for self-love.'

'Cheers, you weirdo.' I smile and close the door behind him. I'd forgotten about the magic stones.

I sit down on the edge of my sofa and tap my feet on the floor, adrenaline still pumping through my veins. Jake's not home for a while and I need something to take my mind off the inevitable confrontation. I scroll through my phone and click on the fashion blogger's message. She's sent me their measurements now after I'd replied saying I was happy to go ahead. Just as I'm reading it my phone dies.

Great.

My laptop's perched on the coffee table so I reach for that and log into Instagram again. Shit. That old thing's died too. There must be a charger somewhere for this, if not I'll go and get the phone charger from the bedroom and stop being so lazy. I scrabble under the TV cabinet for a lead that will fit my laptop when I notice Jake's laptop staring at me, hidden away down the side between the TV unit and the dresser. It's red, shiny and new, he got it just before lockdown, I remember him spending hours on it playing his game before he discovered he could use the TV. His laptop will be faster than mine. I've not used it before but he won't mind, it's tough shit anyway. I open it up and it asks for a password, that's easy as he always uses the same one for everything *Jakeybaby21*.

Result, I'm in. Now to nose on the fashion blogger and influencers' Instagram and browse the web for some fabric, it's so much better on a bigger screen. I can see the detail a lot better, a nice job to take my mind off stuff until Jake gets home. I click on the internet browser and it instantly brings up his saved web pages. Facebook, SpeedMail and Sky Sports.

No more searching. No more searching, Alannah.

It would be so easy to have a little peep right now. I can see from the tabs that he has been automatically logged in to each of his accounts. I should open up a new tab and search for fabric. But before I can stop myself, I've clicked on his SpeedMail. There's no going back now.

I hold my breath.

Scrolling through the emails I notice lots of junk, unopened stuff he should really unsubscribe too like fitness drinks and food companies, sports shops, sports updates, etc. But one email address catches my eye. It's been opened and replied to on several occasions. It's from a personal account **frankiefoolsgold@SpeedMail.com** I click on the last replied to email and there's a succession of back and forth asking about money. *When will they get paid? How much will he pay?*

Frankie's asking for money.

I dig deeper and further back until I reach the first ever email sent by Frankie on the evening we went into lockdown. It has an attachment and in the body of the text it simply reads: *Here's proof, now it's time to start paying.* I click on the attachment and watch it download, my mind racing with possible scenarios. Is he selling drugs? Is that why he's always so off with Beau recently? To keep him at arm's length in case they cross paths on the drugs' scene. Perhaps the money wasn't for his mum but for his drug dealer, he owes him because perhaps he couldn't sell it. No, that's ludicrous, he hates drugs. But I guess you don't have to like drugs or take them to sell them. The attachment finally finishes downloading. It takes a few seconds to compute what I'm looking at. I stare at it in complete and utter shock.

A DNA test.

It's all there in black and white.

The son of a bitch has a secret child.

I click onto his Facebook and search for a Frankie on his friends list before checking his messages. There's no Frankie. I continue to scroll through conversations between his friends and conversations with his mum. I quickly scan through his mum's messages and there's no mention of money. At all. Until I get to something interesting. Again, sent at the start of lockdown from a Francesca Adino. I know instantly by the profile photo who that is. She's sat smiling on her silver, crushed velvet sofa with a little boy sitting on her knee, he's beaming sweetly back at the camera. The little boy has big blue eyes like the sea, not like his mum's dark eyes, but like his dad's. They look just like his dad's. Jake.

I'm sucked into the Frankiecheska vortex, mindlessly scrolling through all of her photo's. There's a photo of the boy playing in a large garden in a beautiful playhouse with a powder pink picket fence. That gorgeous house I saw when I spied them both at the shop that day, appears to be hers, or at least her parents. The front door slams and he's there. I jump so high that the laptop flies off my lap and onto the floor with an almighty crash. It's probably broken now, just like us.

'Um, what the hell are you doing?' Jake demands. 'You've broken my laptop.' He puts his hands on his hips, chest puffed out.

'Oh, have I? Woops.' I give it a little satisfactory kick and the corner of its cover snaps off and falls onto the floor. Cheap.

'Bitch. You shouldn't be on it anyway, it's my laptop. My personal laptop.'

'Oh dear. I don't like being called a bitch.'

Jake's face loses all colour as I glare at him with pure hatred.

'What are you doing?' he gulps.

'No. What have you *been* doing?' I say slowly, through gritted teeth. I stand up, eye-level with him. His big blue eyes avoiding mine. He deflates like a pathetic, old punctured paddling pool before me, I can almost hear the air forcing its way out of him.

'I was going to tell you,' he quacks in a voice I haven't heard him use before. 'I just didn't know how.'

'How cliché.' I tut. 'So, when we had our lovely meal at the start of lockdown and talked about starting a family, you already fucking had one and you knew about it.' I laugh because the rage has made me hysterical. I get so close to him that he has no choice but to look at me. I hope my breath stinks of that packet of pickled onion monster munch I ate earlier. I hope he can taste it. I want to repulse him now.

'No, it's not like that,' he protests.

I poke my finger on his chest with every word I say. 'But it is like that isn't it. It's exactly like that.'

He says nothing. There is nothing he can say. I've seen it all and he knows it.

'You asked for money that night and cried like a baby, all worried for your mummy. I felt so sorry for you. But it wasn't for mummy, was it? It was for her, for your son. You manipulated me and you have been doing so for weeks, months, years. All the while acting like a total arsehole because you were too ashamed to tell me.'

He says nothing. Just nods. Defeated.

'You're pathetic. Beau was right about you. Get the fuck out. You can't live here anymore.'

'Yeah, I gathered that,' he mumbles and starts to retreat back out of the door. That was almost too easy. Why did I wait all these months for that? But no, I want more.

'When and how?' I scream at him and pull him back into the room.

'What's the point. You know now,' he mutters, peeling my hand off his t-shirt.

'I don't care, you owe me that at least. When did this happen? Tell me everything and then you can go.'

'At the start, it was a one-night stand, a mistake. We knew each other from years ago and then one night I went out with the lads and bumped into her. You and I weren't serious then.'

'When?'

'What?'

'When did you go out exactly?'

'I can't remember, it was years ago.'

'Try.'

'Um, when I was away training.'

When we were sending our love letters. My heart sinks. It was all a lie, from day one.

'You were seeing me and her at the same time. I bet you didn't see your mum once, did you? Another lie.

Why is she asking for money and a DNA test now?'

'Her boyfriend left her, moved away. She has no family here and always knew it was me but didn't need me until he left.'

'Wow, what a mug you are,' I spit. Does she really need his money with a house like that?

'He's my boy, I couldn't ignore him once I knew.'

'And you didn't think to tell me, didn't think I'd understand.' Tears begin to bubble in my eyes then burn down my cheeks. I have to blink twice as much to see through them.

'No, I didn't think you would.'

'Why?' I sniff.

'I don't know. Once I knew, it felt different. I fell out of love with you and I didn't know how to get out. I'm sorry.' He looks down at the floor, a small amount of remorse for a huge betrayal.

'You used me,' I scream, ugly crying. My own words scalding me like freshly boiled water.

'I'm sorry,' he repeats, in a much kinder tone than I've heard in months.

He leaves, not looking back and not taking a thing.

I wipe my face with the sleeve of my jumper, trying to pull myself together but failing and wailing as I walk to the bedroom to charge my phone. After a couple of minutes, I send a message to Flynn. Fearful that his response may break my heart even further.

Jake has a child with Cheska. That boy from the supermarket is his son. Did you know?

Chapter Sixteen

I force myself out onto the balcony to get some air, lean my elbows on the balcony bars and hold my heavy head in my hands.

I've left my phone in the bedroom. I want a few minutes not knowing whether Flynn knew or not. My head is banging with the stress of all this.

Jake doesn't love me.

He has a child with someone else.

I don't know how long the noise has been going on for, too lost in my own thoughts and misery. It takes a little while for me to realise what is happening. At first, it's muffled then it's louder, shouting. I lean further over the balcony to get a closer look and for a millisecond consider if I would feel anything if I accidently fell over. I chastise myself for being so dramatic, there are people a lot worse off than me. People have discovered worse things about the people they love or loved. He could have been a murderer, a rapist, but no, he got someone else pregnant when we were falling in love or at least, when I was. The shouting is coming from Flynn and Jake, name calling.

'FUCKING BASTARD,' Flynn's voice booms through Jake's car window.

I watch Jake open his car door and step out of his car. He pulls himself up to his full five feet and nine inches, looking tiny by comparison to Flynn. He must have been sitting in his car for a while not to have driven off yet, probably messaging her, Frankycheska or whatever her name is and making plans for their future. They say a man doesn't leave until he has an excuse to leave, not loving you isn't enough. They leave when something better comes along, when they're pushed.

Pushing.

Which is what Jake is doing to Flynn right now. I watch on in horror as Flynn tries to back off from Jake, who's clumsily throwing big, angry punches at him. Jake makes another big swing for Flynn and misses before managing to catch him off guard with a hard knee to the stomach. Flynn bends over in agony. Vulnerable. All the while I'm shouting for them to stop but they don't seem to hear or care and then I'm running. Running out of the flat and down the stairs as fast as I can into the car park.

I've got to stop this.

Jake has a bloody nose. He looks a state but is still throwing big, aggressive punches. Flynn is doing some sort of martial arts and is blocking every one of Jake's attempts to punch him again like a skilled athlete, while Jake continues to go for him like an angry, deranged bear.

'HEY,' I shout. 'STOP.'

Jake continues to push and punch. Flynn glances at me, continuing to block until he kicks the back of Jake's knee, causing him to collapse. Jake latches onto Flynn and pulls him down on top of him. They're now both on the floor, rolling around like a couple of lager louts having a drunken brawl. This is not real.

'JUST FUCKING STOP,' I scream. Fists clenched. I'm well aware that the neighbours will now be getting the show of their lives. No reality TV will be able to top this. And I must say, I'm playing my part well as the hysterical damsel in distress.

Jake and Flynn halt, rooted to the spot by my powerful screech and reluctantly step back from one another.

'You can have her now, mate,' Jake spits at Flynn.

Flynn stares at me. Startled. Then wipes sweat off his forehead with his t-shirt.

'I don't know what you're on about mate.'

'Oh, I think you do, *mate*, you've always fancied her. It's fucking obvious. You couldn't bear me being with her which is why you're such a weirdo when she's around.' Jake laughs his spiteful, donkey braying laugh, but it sounds more reedy than usual because he's so out of breath. He looks me up and down in disgust and sneers.

'Whatever you say. Well I know one thing. I wouldn't have treated her the way you have.'

'Yeah, course not. You just go about shagging other women when you've got a bombshell like Becky at home. Don't make out you're a saint because we both know full well, you're not.' Jake's words sting as my eyes dart to Flynn.

'What?' Flynn snaps. His face burning with anger.

'Yeah, I bumped into her. She told me what you did. He's a shady one this one, Alannah.' Jake flicks a thumb up, pointing directly at Flynn.

'That's not true. Whatever she said, it's not true,' Flynn protests.

'Well, sounds pretty true to me. So, who's worse now? MATE,' Jake scoffs.

'Did you know?' I hear myself asking Flynn. 'Did you know about him and Cheska?' Now it's my turn to finger point.

'No, Alannah. I promise. The first time I'd seen her since we worked together twelve years ago was in the supermarket that day in the egg aisle. And that shit about Becky isn't true. You know the truth.' Something in his eyes is pleading with me. Jake doesn't know about Becky and her toy boy getting caught out in the car park. Flynn doesn't want him to know. 'She's just trying to save face and reflect it back onto me. I'd never do that.'

'Is she?' I say quietly, my throat raw with emotion. Flynn wouldn't do that, or would he? Can I really trust anyone anymore?

'Yes.' Flynn nods his head slowly, looking forlorn.

The hairs on the back of my neck stand on end. Out of the corner of my eye I catch Jake walking backwards to his car, reaching for the driver's door. Trying to make a sly getaway.

'I want my money back,' I blurt out. But he just ignores me. 'Every penny,' I continue, stepping closer to him, blocking his car door. 'By the end of next month. Or I'll ring your mum and tell her everything. How you lied to get what you want and used her as a decoy. I might tell Cheska too. See what she makes of it, you disgusting pig.'

'No, you won't. Cheska can't stand you, you'd be wasting your breath.'

'How can she not stand me? She doesn't even know who I am.'

'Yeah she does. After that day in the supermarket, she looked you up on Facebook. She told me everything by the way. Her version of events was very different to yours.'

'Well she must know me really well if she's looked me up on Facebook,' I reply sarcastically, folding my arms.

'You ripped the eggs out of her hands right after she told you that she really needed them to make a birthday cake for MY boy. You're a heartless bitch and my boy saw everything. I'm so glad we didn't have a child together.'

'SO AM I,' I scream 'Your boy!? The boy you didn't even know about until a few months ago. I dodged a massive bullet not starting a family with you. Go and play happy fucking families with Cheska, you piece of shit.' The words come out smoothly but they hurt like knives afterwards as I gulp down a painful lump in my throat.

Jake looks back at me, composed and smirking. He's pure evil. They deserve each other. Ripping eggs out of her hands, how dare she. I should have cracked the lot over her head, there and then. Flynn marches over to Jake and grabs him by the scruff of the neck. I step back and take deep breaths, trying to calm myself down. This is so humiliating.

'It's time for you to go now,' Flynn orders, pushing Jake back into his car as he stumbles into the driver's seat. He lands on the horn with a massive HONK. Well, if the neighbours weren't already watching, they will certainly be curtain twitching now.

'Gladly,' Jake says with a sneer, pushing Flynn off. He shuffles into his seat, turns on the ignition and speeds off down the road without a second look.

Flynn and I stand there like a couple of zombies out of Jake's computer game. A game, because this is all it was to Jake. A game to see how much he could get out of me before he ran away to her. I'm shocked at how quickly he made a decision, maybe it was always her and he was just waiting for his chance. I didn't know him at all.

'Are you okay? Here,' Flynn finally speaks and passes me some antibacterial hand gel.

'Not a lot of good that will do now,' I croak as I take the bottle from him anyway and squirt some gel into my hands. I pass it back to him. He squirts out a massive blob onto his hands then rubs it all over his hands, face and body, wincing at it stings his skin. Disinfecting every inch of Jake's angry jabs. I want to do the same. I want to shower in disinfectant then take my brain out and disinfect that too, erase all memory of him.

What an utter waste of my time.

'I shouldn't have laid a finger on him I know. It's stupid,' Flynn says. 'I've never had a fight in my life, least of all with someone who is meant to be a mate. But I've seen you suffering all these months and I couldn't believe it when I saw your text. Then I happened to look out of the window and there he was, sitting in his car smiling and chatting on his phone. Something just took over. I had to say something.'

'And punch him,' I add, looking up at him, a small smile playing across my lips.

'Hey, it was self-defence.'

'I know. His nose was a mess,' I agree, widening my eyes. 'It was quite satisfying to see. Am I a horrible person?' I ask.

'Nope, not at all. It's probably broken but he'll get over it. Listen, about what Jake said, I…'

'Hey guys, what's going down?' Beau interrupts as he approaches us with Laura in tow. They look like they've been to the beach. Towels draped around their bodies, their hair wet and shaggy. So that's who he's been meeting all this time. Sly brother. 'Sis, you look like shit. Oh. What's happened?' Beau's expression changes from piss-take to protective brother as he clocks my swollen, red eyes.

'Oh, Alannah,' Laura says frowning, with concern.

'Wow, do I really look that bad? I wasn't even the one in a fight.'

'Fight?? I missed a fight!' Beau jumps up and down, limbs everywhere. His towel falls from his waist revealing rainbow coloured swim shorts with ducks on them. I catch Flynn trying not to laugh.

'Pipe down puppy, you're meant to be a lover not a fighter,' Laura simpers, looking at Beau with gooey eyes.

'I am, sweetness, for you I'm the lover but sometimes a man needs to fight for his rights.' Beau nods enthusiastically at Laura then shadow boxes the air a few times. 'I take it you confronted him then? But why the fight?' Beau and Laura look at us both expectantly.

'Jake had a baby,' I announce. It sounds so strange to hear myself say that.

'Huh?' Beau and Laura say in unison.

'Jake fathered a baby at the start of our relationship, when we were in the honeymoon stage. The child is five now. The mother's bloke left her so she tracked Jake down just before lockdown for a DNA test, just trying her luck. I expect she didn't know whose it was, but she got the result she wanted anyway and has been making him pay ever since. Well, I've been paying as I thought I was helping Jake's mum with money because she lost her job, turns out I was paying his child maintenance for him,' I say matter of factly and shrug my shoulders. It feels weirdly therapeutic to say it out loud.

'What an utter CU…' Beau begins but stops mid-sentence at Laura's glare.

'Beau,' Laura says gently, her eyes wide. She's keeping him in check already.

'I mean, what a dick. A baby with who?' Beau continues.

'That bitch from the supermarket. The one I told you about. I saw them together remember, arguing at the shop. Probably about money. I stopped paying him when his mum got a job and then he was out personal training all the time, trying to make the money up, I expect.'

'Christ on a bike,' Beau remarks.

'Oh, Alannah, I'm so sorry,' Laura adds.

'So why are *you* fighting with him?' Beau asks Flynn. 'OHHHHHH, you two.' Beau giggles and starts pointing between me and Flynn. He can be so embarrassing at times. And childish.

'NO. I thought Flynn knew about it as he used to know Cheska. He didn't know but when he found out, he confronted Jake too. Well, they had a fight, Jake's got a broken nose,' I explain, shutting Beau down immediately. The last thing I need is Beau matchmaking.

'Ahh right.' Beau eyes us both suspiciously. 'Nice one, Flynn. I knew he was up to something, didn't I, Alannah?' Beau nods his head at Flynn with approval.

'Yep, you did. Listen guys, this has been fun and all that.' I smile and swallow down another painful emotional gulp. 'But I think I'm going to go and have a lay down. I've got a headache.' My voice sounds way sadder than my face probably looks.

'Give me a call when you wake up,' Laura says. 'We can go for a walk, a whinge and a wine, I'll go and get some now.'

'Thanks Laura, I'll let you know if I'm up to it.' I offer a small wave and smile at everyone. I walk back up to my flat, legs like lead as I trudge up the stairs.

I get inside the flat, into bed, then sob uncontrollably until I pass out.

Chapter Seventeen

Almost fifteen weeks since the start of lockdown – 4th July – hairdressers, pubs and restaurants are due to open. People can meet in the house with another household or six separate people from separate households outside.

'Hi Judy. Wait there. I'll go and grab everything.'

Jake's mum is here at the flat, she's been sent round to pick up his stuff. He obviously can't bear to face me and I'm relieved not to have to see him but also equally uncomfortable to face his mum. It's been almost three weeks since I found out about the secret love child but this is the first time he's attempted to collect his things, even if not in person. I imagine him wearing the same boxers every day for all that time. The thought makes me shudder, but it wouldn't surprise me. I bet he's grown that tramp beard again too. Or maybe not if he's trying to win Frankycheska back.

There are still lots of unanswered questions. Was it a one-night stand? Or was it more than that? Whatever it was, it has got to be when we first met and were falling in love, if my maths is right that fits with the birthday of their boy. A memory of one-night pings into my mind, he was away training and came home at the weekend, he was supposed to be staying with me after a night out with the lads but he didn't. Instead, he sent a text saying he was going home as he was super tired. I bet it was that night they bumped uglies. I was binned off for a shag with the stunning Frankycheska. That thought makes me despise them both even more, they deserve each other. I'll probably never know what truly happened, I doubt Jake will ever tell me so I should just forget it and not torture myself with the facts. But I can't forget it, I need to know.

'Okay love, you just take your time,' Judy replies with a blank expression on her face. I can't read her eyes, the fact that I can't see her mouth due to the mask she's wearing probably doesn't help either. She's normally the first one to say what an idiot her son is being but she isn't giving anything away today. I pad back into the flat and grab his bin bags of clothes, and a few plastic boxes full of odd plates and cutlery that I don't need and he can have. I've had a clear out and I've basically given him all the shit. He'll be cussing me later. The box with the letters in, is going back too so he can be reminded of them and feel guilty. I've written him another letter, nothing bitter, just a goodbye to add to his collection. I wonder when he'll find it. Maybe Frankycheska will, that would be good.

'Here, you go. I think that's everything. Let me know if I've missed anything,' I speak like I'm talking to one of my customers. Because I have quite a few of them now, more than I'd like in fact but I mustn't complain, even if it is extremely overwhelming.

'Thanks, Alannah, I will do,' she answers, shifting on her feet from side to side. Her eyes squinting. She's still standing here.

'I'm sorry he sent you, this must be awkward for you too,' I say to fill the awkward silence. This must be hard for Judy; we got on well.

'Oh no, I wanted to come by, love. I wanted to see you. He's told me about the money and I'll pay you back every month if that's okay, until he's squared you off.' She continues to shift on her feet.

'O-k-a-y, but it's Jake who owes me the money. You shouldn't be paying me.' I'm annoyed that he's managed to manipulate her too.

'I know, love. I want to. I'm helping him, I've got to, I'm his mum. Thanks for lending him the money, it's been dire straits for us all, hasn't it?'

'Okay, fair enough,' I mutter. Oh no, Jake. Oh no you don't get away with this.

'I'm sorry it's come to this; you'll always be the daughter I never had.' Judy's sniffs, her eyes welling up.

'Me too. I'm sorry too.' I well up with her then quickly blink the tears away. I don't want to get upset and for it to get reported back to him.

'Um, would it be really cheeky to ask for a spare TV? I only have one at my house and we don't watch the same things,' she says, looking embarrassed. 'I can give it back after he's bought a new one.' She quickly adds.

'Zombies?' I ask, raising an eyebrow.

'Yes.' She blows air out of her cheeks. Relieved.

'Of course.' I smile at her knowingly and scoot back into the house. I'm in there for a while fumbling with the box and the leads until I finally manage to stuff it all in. I bring out the TV that she bought for me. It's tainted now anyway and there's only one of me so what use are two TV's?

'Thank you, I'll buy a TV soon so you can have this one back.

'No, keep it.'

'Oh, but Alannah that was a gift. Are you sure?' She grimaces but I can tell she is pleased as punch about keeping the TV. It's a small mercy for having to live with Jake again. Poor woman. She will be doing everything for him apart from wiping his bum.

'I'm sure. So have you met him yet? Your grandson?' I carefully move the TV box closer towards her on the floor, using it as an excuse to avert eye contact.

'Grandson' Judy repeats but I'm not sure if it sounds like a question.

'The money I was paying Jake that I thought was going to you, was going towards maintenance for his son. You knew that, right?' I'm being naughty now, but if he's told her the truth then it won't matter.

'Oh yes, of course, no, no love. I haven't met him. When the time is right,' she says with a false cheeriness to her tone, head bobbing from side to side. My stomach flips for her, I'm being incredibly petty.

A woman scorned.

'What did he tell you Judy? About us?'

Judy pauses and thinks for a second and then opens her mouth to speak.

'He said you grew apart and that you both wanted different things, you wanted a family and he didn't. Is that not true?' She looks at me pleadingly, searching for something, anything that will tell her that her son isn't a complete arsehole.

'Yes, that's true. I wanted a family, just turns out he already had one. Everyone makes mistakes,' I offer with a shrug and Judy shakes her head.

'Well thanks for the stuff, take care of yourself and enjoy not having to endure hours of zombie killing,' Judy chirps quickly. She probably wants to go home and ask Jake what the hell I'm talking about. I bet she's weirdly excited at the prospect of a grandson, little does she know she has missed the first five years of his life. I feel sad for her.

'I will. Take care, Judy.' I watch her start to walk off then she looks back at me again and speaks. 'You deserve better, love. I knew he was up to something when he kept reminding me not to talk to you about my job and in fact to leave you alone all together, said it would upset you too much because you had lost your job and had a lot going on.' She shakes her head in disbelief. So, she didn't know. He was playing her too.

'Well he did a good job keeping us apart. If only I'd called you, we all would have been out of the dark a lot sooner.'

'Hindsight is a wonderful thing, my love. He sounds like he has a lot of growing up to do, don't worry I'll be kicking his bum into action. He'll be back begging to be with you in no time,' she offers. Hopeful. My nose makes a weird snorting noise and I stifle it with a sad smile. Never in a million years would I take him back. No way. But it doesn't stop me being devastatingly sad about everything.

'Doubt it, but thanks, Judy. Bye,' I force out my squeaky reply as I wave her off.

Watching her go, I swallow down big gulps of guilt. I shouldn't have said anything. Why couldn't I behave demurely and let Judy find out for herself? No, I had to act bitter and now I've upset Judy and wound myself up. Double whammy.

I'm so angry.

I march out onto the balcony to get some air; the woman below is out on her balcony singing a Billie Holiday song which is unusual for her as it's normally her own painful creations or something super squeaky and poppy. She's singing *No Good Man*, how fitting. It's as though she's listened to our conversation and is now doing the sound track. I listen to her sing about not being treated right and the guy spending his money foolishly, and I scoff to myself. He's spending my money on his love child.

I'm the fool.

Jake and I always used to listen to Billie Holiday. I plonk down into the seat and sob. I sob for my old life and the uncertainty of my new one. I sob for us and what we used to be; I mourn the old Jake. Tears stream down my cheeks like a power shower.

Sometimes I'll be doing something completely mundane like washing the dishes or cleaning my teeth and the tears will just come out of nowhere, it's like a strange kind of grief. He isn't dead but he may as well be to me, I'm probably never going to see him again. Who am I kidding? I live in Coolsbay, of course I'll see him again. I'll probably bump into the whole happy family on a cosy little outing to the supermarket. I knew I was losing him way before I knew about Cheska but now it's reality and it really, really sucks big hairy balls.

The sobs are coming harder and faster now. I haven't cried for four days and I was proud of my achievement but now it seems I'm making up for it in bucket loads. The sleeves of my top are being used to wipe the tears off my face with big aggressive swooping motions, sleeves sopping wet and soggy now. My vision is blurry, I need to sort myself out. Get a tissue.

Do something.

Flynn appears on his balcony waving frantically at me whilst the singing woman changes her song to Nina Simone, *Feeling Good*. Hmm she's not got the sound track right anymore. I watch him pick up something from his balcony table and use it like a control. He's trying to point at something with his head, jolting himself backwards and forwards like an excited dolphin. What is that? Oh, it appears to be a little drone, I think, and it's heading for me.

Flynn's attached something to it. It could be a note. I squint my eyes to try and get a better look as it veers to the left and then straightens up to my eye level. No, it's tissues. Tissues for my soggy face. I laugh despite my misery, as snot shoots out of my nose. Singing woman belts out a verse from Nina. The lyrics are a little more apt this time. It is a new dawn and it is a new day and I'm not feeling good but I know I will get better, in time I will. I have to.

With my arms outstretched, I get up and try to position myself in a good place to catch the drone. It's taking a while to get here, swaying this way and that. My eyes are on the prize. Flynn looks as if he is holding his breath. Concentration working overtime, his tongue poking out of the side of his mouth and eyes squinting as his body leans in unison with the drone.

'THAT'S IT, A LITTLE TO THE LEFT,' I shout. It's so close. Hands outstretched; I can almost touch it with my fingertips.

'NO, NO. A BIT MORE TO THE RIGHT. CAN YOU BRING IT FORWARD A BIT?'

'IT WON'T DO IT,' Flynn shouts back, tapping away frantically on the controls. The drone thinks about it, hovers for two seconds then makes a strange, deep groaning noise. It doesn't want to come near me. My miserable presence is repelling all gestures of goodwill.

'OH NO, COMEEE BACK,' I wail as the little drone rattles, reverses and starts heading off towards the maisonettes. This drone is on a whole new mission.

'NOOOOOOO,' Flynn hollers. 'NOOOOOOOOO. ARRGHHHHH,' he booms again as he completely loses control of the feisty little drone. We both watch on, baffled. Flynn's expression changes to horror as the drone takes on a mind of its own.

'NOT IN THERE, ANYWHERE BUT THERE,' Flynn roars. This drone knows exactly where it wants to go and it's not to my balcony.

'COME BACK YOU LITTLE SHIT.' Flynn's fingers work desperately as he clicks on the controls to try and summon back his drone. His efforts are lost as it lazily picks its landing spot. Right above the baldy man's garden. That's right, the baldy man that gave himself a colonic with his garden hose. The drone does one final little tease to Flynn by making loud whirring noises and wobbling itself from side the side. It really looks like it might change its mind and fly back to me. But no. It's on its final descent to the ground. In an attempt to divert the drone, Flynn helplessly chucks the remote at it. He misses and the remote lands in the Baldy man's garden bush, right before the drone crash lands in the middle of his garden dumping shredded tissue everywhere. The only saving grace is that Baldy man isn't there to witness it happen but what will he think when he sees it? Flynn pulls at his hair with his fingers and stares at me in disbelief. I cover my mouth with my hands, trying desperately not to giggle but my shoulders do the talking as they jig up and down.

'THANK YOU. THAT'S CHEERED ME UP A TREAT,' I screech to Flynn through my hysterics.

He looks up and smiles, the biggest, warmest of smiles.

Chapter Eighteen

The next month goes by in a bit of a busy blur as work is really taking off.

It's fairly quiet in terms of seeing people (mainly because I don't have the time to shit) apart from a flying visit from Beau and Laura who are sickeningly loved up. I told Beau he could have chosen a better time to get a girlfriend than right during my breakup, he just laughed and told me it's not all about me and forced another stone into my hand. This time a green one, Aventurine, apparently for creativity. He's right I guess, but I can't help feeling a little sorry for myself and irrationally annoyed at him for being so inconsiderate.

I do feel better though, something's shifted.

My thoughts aren't consumed with grief for our relationship anymore, I have my moments still but I definitely feel better. Mum also came over which was lovely and we had a proper catch up. I mustered up the courage to tell her about me and Jake and she couldn't believe it. She was very supportive but chuckled at my supermarket show down and even more so at the fight between Jake and Flynn. Like an episode out of a bloody soap opera, she'd said, whilst spitting out her tea. Life is slowly returning to normal, but not the normal I knew. My new normal.

Flynn. Apart from a quick wave across the balconies, I haven't seen him since the drone flew into baldy guy's garden. He's probably avoiding me and all my dramas. I miss him. We have been messaging each other though, his texts always cheer me up. He sends a funny meme most mornings to help brighten my day. I look forward to those messages more than he knows.

I slump down on the sofa for a well-deserved coffee break after sewing solidly for five hours for all my new customers and grab my phone off the coffee table.

Time to finally message Daniel back. But it's been so long, is it even worth it? No, better late than never. Let's get this done.

Me: *Hi Daniel, so sorry it's taken me ages to reply. The thing is I've just broken up with my boyfriend after learning some horrible news about him. I think it's best we just remain friends. I hope that's okay.*

Now I don't work at Emmanuel's, I'll probably never see him again as he doesn't live in Coolsbay, but that's probably good for me. The last thing I need is another man to get disillusioned by.

Just me, myself and I. A spinster forever, that suits me fine.

I click onto my Instagram, then onto the fashion blogger's Instagram page with my dresses and sigh heavily at the number of requests for a matching tea-dress and mask. I then let out a noise somewhere between a sigh and a groan that sounds like a demented seal as I take in my living room. It's a total mess. There's fabric everywhere. Don't get me wrong, I'm over the moon that there's this much interest but I don't really know where to start. Making those three dresses and masks for the fashion blogger and influencers was a big enough job in itself as they wanted them as soon as possible and it had to be perfect. I'm just not sure if I can keep the momentum up. Help is required. I rack my brains again for the fiftieth time this week, mum has offered to help for a bit but I'd have to give her back her sewing machine and buy my own. I'll do that with my next payback instalment from Jake's mum.

One other person helping just isn't enough though. I've had to tell the Coolsbay scrub hub that I can't help them anymore. They were so cool about it and said not to worry as orders were beginning to slow down now anyway.

Coolsbay scrub hub... could I ask them?

I don't know how I didn't think of this before. I didn't really interact with the other girls at Coolsbay as it was all done from home, apart from bumping into the occasional person when we picked up our material. But, I do get on well with Mandy, she could round up the others. I quickly draft an email on my phone to Mandy who runs the scrub hub then delete it almost immediately. The wording is all wrong. I need to be a little vague, just put the feelers out there to see if she's willing to help first and tempt them in by mentioning payment as I'll have to pay them, obviously. I'm so desperate not to disappoint or upset the customers that I even consider paying the scrub hub teams and doing it for free but I don't put this in my email to Mandy of course. I might have to work for cheap or even free at first if I'm thinking of the bigger picture. But of course, I wouldn't expect the girls to work for free. Most of them have never even met me for a start and those that have, it was just fleeting. There has to be something in it for them too. The whole thing sets my nerves on fire. I could be doing all of this for nothing but I guess I'll never know unless I try. I shudder at the thought of no one being able to help and having some very angry, disappointed customers on my hands, no doubt vocalising it all on social media. I slurp down the rest of my coffee and lay back to stare at my ceiling. My reputation in the fashion industry could be tarnished forever. I can't mess this up. I take a deep breath and start the email again to Mandy. *If you don't ask, you don't get*, Bet's voice echoes in my head. She's right.

Email to Mandy, sent.

I wake up hours later on the sofa, confused and with dribble running out of the corner of my mouth. Shit, I haven't got time for cat naps. Mandy hasn't replied and neither has Daniel, not surprised about Daniel really. I feel really silly for responding, should have just left it. Urgh. I feel gross. In fact, I actually feel hungover which is weird because I haven't drunk anything for weeks. Alcohol just doesn't agree with me when I'm feeling down so it's best to leave it out altogether. This must be what stress does to you, you pass out from the anxiety of it all.

I peel myself off the sofa and go and make my fourth cup of coffee today coupled with some fruit in an attempt to look after myself. Normally I'd have a blueberry muffin or something similar but I'm taking care of me. Self-love. The pink stone that Beau gave me glistens on the kitchen window sill, he told me to cleanse it as it's been in the house with Jake so has probably picked up a lot of negative energy. '*Cleanse it in sea salt and water and then leave it on the window sill for a full moon or sunlight to do its work. Get rid of all those nasty vibes, man,'* he'd said. I felt a bit silly but I thought I better do it or I'll only get a lecture about how I'm not helping myself.

I scoff down another banana as they are particularly miniscule and then hold the pink stone in my hand. Rose quartz I think he said it's called. It feels warm and smooth in my palm, I wonder if it actually does anything.

The doorbell rings, making me jump. I put the stone down on the side and pad down to the door to see who it is. Peering through my brand-new shiny spyhole that Beau fitted, I see someone holding a huge bunch of flowers with a big smile pasted on his face.

Oh my God.

It's Daniel.

I have summoned him with the powers of the stone.

No. No. No. No. This is not happening.

I glance in the mirror by the door and shake my head at my reflection. My hair, resembles that of a cockatiel and I have big tram lines all over my face from the sofa cushions. That stone is having a laugh. I use my hands to smooth down my hair and pinch my cheeks to give them some colour, like I'm a 1930s housewife, because why not? I don't want a relationship with the man, but I also don't want to look like I've just stepped out of an asylum. He is still hot, after all.

'Hey, Daniel. This is a nice, um, surprise,' I say, opening the door and not sounding too convincing. My bad face and hair are making me feel very self-conscious.

'Hey, Alannah. So pleased to see you, these are for you, doll,' Daniel replies, grinning and pushing the big bunch of flowers into my hands.

'Thanks. They're beautiful.' I take them from him and breath in their aroma. Awkward, but I'm grateful I now have something to hide my face behind. Sadly, there is no vase in the flat anymore. It went back to Jake as it was just a reminder of him and the few times he bought me flowers when he'd done something wrong. Stupid. I gave him back loads of things that I could really do with now.

'Listen,' he smiles and rubs his stubble with his hand. 'I got your text and thought I'd come and visit. See you face to face. There's some things I wanted to say…' he continues. He's still talking but I'm not hearing any of it. My heart races.

Flynn has just appeared behind him and is now backing away as we lock eyes. His big puppy-dog eyes look intense, surprised and hurt. I open my mouth to say something but nothing comes out and before I know it, he's gone again. What must this look like? A guy he's never seen before at my door with a huge bunch of flowers. Daniel hasn't even noticed and is still babbling away, about Zeze or something.

'Sorry Daniel, I'm so tired I zoned out, what were you saying?' I mumble, feeling suddenly sad.

'How rude.' He chuckles, not phased at all.

'I came to tell you that I'm going back to Manchester in a few weeks. I've been offered a job back home. I just thought you might be up for a bit of fun before, but if you're still heartbroken then it might not be a good idea but then again it might take your mind off it.' He watches my face with a hint of a naughty grin and a twinkle in his eye. I hide behind the flowers even more so and clear my throat.

'Yeah. Probably not a good idea and especially with what's going on,' I say flatly. I told him I just wanted to be friends but he clearly just wanted fun. How naive of me. He probably has a whole hareem of women just for fun.

'Of course,' he replies, with his hands in his pockets and his legs in a wide stance. 'Hey, I've got some more news about Zeze if you want to hear it.' His eyes twinkle again.

'Oh God, I don't know if I do want to hear it,' I say, sounding hoarse. 'I hope she hasn't been caught out abusing more people. Poor Lance.'

'No no, nothing like that.' Daniel shakes his head.

'What is it then?' Now I'm intrigued.

'Well, she faked pretty much her whole C.V. She had no experience at all in fashion retail. And, she's been in prison. Someone from her old job contacted Manni and dobbed her in. They thought he should know as she'd tracked Zeze down and found out what she was doing for work. Probably a former disgruntled co-worker.'

'Ahh, your sources from HR not acting so HR again. Okay, now I'm listening.' I carefully put down the flowers on the small table by the door then fold my arms.

'You're so cheeky.' Daniel smiles.

I'm shocked but also slightly impressed that she managed to wing it for this long. No experience in fashion retail, but it all makes sense now. I listen intently as Daniel reveals Zeze's dark past.

Ten years ago, Zeze worked for a car dealership in South Wales. She withdrew money over a four-year period whilst working as an account assistant, manipulating financial systems to cover seventy-one transactions made to her personal bank accounts. Zeze was only caught out after she had worked there for six years when she went on holiday and the irregularities came to light via the financial controller. She was sent down for five years but let out after two and a half for good behaviour, she admitted embezzling a total of £168,253 from the dealership. Zeze forged and falsified documents and manipulated the accounts of the company in an attempt to cover her activities and avoid detection. She created credit notes that showed outstanding payments from the dealership, but the money was going directly into her bank account. In her defence, Zeze stated her mother was severely ill and she didn't know what to do, hence the embezzling, she wanted to pay for her to go private and get well again. Her lies were exposed quickly, everyone knows treatment on the NHS is free and usually very fast if it is needed. It also turns out her mother wasn't even ill; she's been estranged from her for many years. It was all big fat lies.

When I saw her in the supermarket, she was still using her mother being ill as a lie, an excuse to get away perhaps. People are so weird. Before she got caught, Zeze used the money to buy herself many luxuries including a boob job and a tummy tuck. The irony is you would certainly never know she'd had either of those things done now.

It was hardly worth it.

'Wow. A fraudster and a fondler,' I comment and Daniel chuckles.

'I know, you just never know some people and what secrets they keep right?'

'You honestly don't, Daniel,' I agree.

You really don't.

Chapter Nineteen

Early September 2020 – six months since the UK entered lockdown. All children have returned to school and most people have returned to work.

Michael: *Dear Alannah, thank you for your note and kind words. Mum was always an inspiration to all of us and if it wasn't for her then I wouldn't be living in Australia right now. She gave me the courage to go for it. I'm so sorry it's taken me months to reply. I wasn't able to attend the funeral due to the virus and planes not being able to enter or leave Australia. Neither was my sister, as she also lives down here. Mum's death really did hit me hard. The only people that were allowed to go were family so that was just my brother (who lives in Birmingham) and his family. I'm so sorry that you weren't able to say your final goodbyes as well. I do remember mum telling me about you. You were getting into making dresses, weren't you? Are they the ones posted on your social media with the matching masks? They are awesome. I actually own a boutique clothes shop down here where I live in the little suburb of Mooloolaba, as well as run a hair salon with my wife. If you ever fancy a trip to Australia you should come and visit us. My wife and I will be more than happy to show you the sites of the Sunshine Coast, when this is all over, of course.*

Me: *Michael. It's great to hear from you. It seems these unusual circumstances we're in are making painfully sad events even more difficult. It must have been so upsetting and frustrating not to be able to attend your mum's funeral. I was upset too but I can't imagine how it must have felt for you guys. Yes, I have been getting into making dresses and matching masks. It's actually become a little more than a hobby now. I'm making pieces for actual customers, so I am really chuffed. I would be more than happy to send you a couple of sample dresses for your shop, if you'd like them. I've googled Mooloolaba, it looks absolutely stunning. The thought of a holiday seems like a dream right now, albeit a distant one. Thank you so much for your kind invitation. I may just take you and your wife up on that one day.*
Alannah

I log out of Facebook and close my laptop after virtually visiting the Sunshine Coast for over an hour. I'm so desperate to get away and just relax. As soon as the girls are trained up and happy, and it's safe, that's it. I'm booking a flight out of here to Mooloolaba. I'll have to go alone I expect, but I don't care, I'm in love with it already. I guess in a way it resembles Coolsbay, a sleepy small, seaside town with lots of character and tons of quirky small businesses. The difference is that the weather is way better than here and it looks much trendier and younger too.

Time to stretch the legs.

I peel myself off the sofa and stroll down to the beach, it's much quieter and cleaner now the kids have gone back to school and people are returning to their jobs after months of being furloughed or working from home. Being furloughed didn't last long for me, it was less than two months and then I was made redundant. The memory of the Zoom call with Manni still plays over in my mind. I managed to keep it together until Manni uncharacteristically cried on me, I felt so sad for him. The business that he'd spent so long building up from scratch has had to be stripped right back, it may never be the same again. He looked tired, older and way more serious.

Manni said very kind words to me about my work at Emmanuel's and much to my own surprise I ended up telling him all about my new venture. He was so delighted for me and stressed that if I wanted any advice then to please ask him. That was good to hear, I'm pleased we had the call in the end and it ended the way it did. It was definitely my time to leave. I wonder how long I would have stayed at Emmanuel's if lockdown had never happened. I wonder if Jake would still be here, Cheska may not had ever entered our lives if her boyfriend hadn't decided to leave her and who knows why he left.

The butterfly effect – Jake and I could still be together.

My body shudders at the thought, lockdown has been hard and traumatic for many but it's unlocked a lot more opportunities for me and freed me of a fake relationship. I feel strangely liberated.

The warm sea air tickles my nostrils as I inhale slowly through my nose then exhale out through my mouth. I come to the beach most days on the off chance I might bump into Flynn doing a beach clear up but I haven't seen him for ages. He hasn't been replying to my messages either. The amusing meme's have stopped, ever since he saw me with Daniel. I know he's doing really well from snooping at him on social media. It looks like he's got more promotional jobs for sportswear. It's funny, he never talked about it. I think he's one of those people where things like that just come easy to him. People are just drawn to him.

After a brief scope around for Flynn and more big inhales of head-clearing sea air, I leave the beach and make my way to the high street to get a coffee from the bakery. I've been coming here a lot since it re-opened. It's become part of my new daily routine. Wake up, get dressed, check emails, check in on the girls and their work, go for a walk and get coffee, then sew until I drop. The door dings as I walk through it and I'm greeted by Gloria's warm smile.

'Hello, Alannah, same as usual?' she asks as she finishes serving another customer.

'Yes please, Gloria. How are you this morning?'

'Really good thanks, lovely. Trade is picking up really well now.' She gives me a big grin. She looks so well. Just before lockdown Gloria looked tired, run down and had a strange limp to go with it, she told me she'd injured herself gardening but couldn't take time off to rest so it could heal. Well, lockdown had other plans for her, just like it did for me. That's all vanished, she appears as fit as a fiddle and glows with happiness. The shop has been updated too. She tells me her whole family pulled together over lockdown and invested a bit of blood, sweat and tears into it. They refreshed the menu and contacted all of the local businesses giving them a discount if they booked a lunchtime collection box. The break from normal life was what her and her business needed.

'That's great news, Gloria and I'm not surprised considering what you've done with the place. It's looks amazing.' I look around at what was once a tired, magnolia and brown painted bakery. It's now painted a crisp white with a brick affect wall paper behind the counter, the dressers and shelves have also been painted white. The name *Gloria's* is painted in duck egg blue italics across the top of the dressers which matches the new glossy sign out the front of the bakery. It looks gorgeous.

'Thanks, lovely.' Gloria hands me my latte and croissant and I take my usual seat by the window. I like to spy on Emmanuel's because the window display makes me feel a little smug.

The first time I saw it I couldn't quite believe it; in fact, I was so pissed off that I had to stop myself from storming in there and demanding they take it down. Now I just find it funny and quite sweet. It's a compliment to me and also a bit worrying that they couldn't come up with their own ideas and had to use mine. Because it is all my idea, the idea I came up with in six minutes.

I watch Cherry buzz around the shop, quacking demands at the poor staff. Then I scrutinise the display again. It's not exactly how I would have done it but it still looks good. There are four mannequins in beautiful summer dresses, rich in colour and floor length, apart from one which sits just above the knee. Each mannequin is holding a cocktail in her hand. The background is that of a garden, with lovely, white wrought iron garden furniture and an archway covered in gorgeous, light pink roses. The mannequins are having a wonderful time, happy and carefree in their stunning dresses while one of them, the one in the short dress, shows off her garden.

Cherry clocks me watching and instantly turns

beetroot. I can't help but smile and wave at her like she's an old friend. She flinches, then her already tiny mouth shrinks down to cat bum hole size. She flicks her hair and sticks her nose up in the air. I'm not quite sure why she's acting like that, maybe I'm putting her off watching her every day and being on her patch. Or perhaps Zeze has said things about me to her, belittled my work in that store. Well more fool her for believing what Zeze says, the fraudster, the fondler.

I *should* stop snooping, it's just for my own amusement anyway and it would upset Manni if he knew I was taunting the new manager, even though I am just looking in the shop window and smiling. It doesn't take much to wind some people up.

I finish my latte and thank Gloria before trundling home to sew. This evening I'm actually going out for drinks with Laura and Beau. I'm extra excited as tomorrow I'm giving myself the day off to lay around, watch crap on TV and just generally revel in being lazy. I've been working solidly for months now and I deserve to have a little fun, plus the girls have relieved me of some of the workload. Mandy was so helpful and I managed to get four girls on board to help me out with sewing, I'm paying them, not loads but more than I'm paying myself at the moment and they can fit it around their day jobs. Once I get the next batch of dresses out, I'll be able to give myself and the girls a little bonus too. It's all working out quite well.

♥ ♥ ♥

My flat is looking rather nice now after my mammoth tidy up. I breath in through my nose then let the air out of my mouth slowly before twirling around in my living room in my new dress. I pour myself a glass of white wine and then wait for my guests to arrive. The woman below is singing so I go outside onto the balcony to listen a bit more. I've quite gotten used to her now and I even ask for the odd request which she is more than happy to do. Right now, she's singing something by Paloma Faith and it's a good one.

I can see Flynn pottering around in his living room, I consider waving but then I stoop down in my chair so he can't see me looking. He appears to be tidying up, plumping up cushions on the sofa and doing something to his dinner table which sits by the window just like mine. He's dressed up too, wearing smart jeans and a patterned Hawaiian looking shirt. His hair's been cut, short at the sides, sitting thick and wavy on the top of his head. I sigh at the sight of him. Such a vision of pure loveliness. I've well and truly buggered that up.

I think back to Daniel's impromptu visit and the look on Flynn's face when he saw me with the flowers. The penny finally dropped then that Flynn may have feelings for me and I may have been trying to dismiss mine. I want to talk to him about it and explain but at the same time I don't want to assume anything. He could just be giving me a wide berth as he thinks I have a new boyfriend.

Flynn catches me watching him as I've unwittingly sat back up straight to get a better look. I give a little wave; he does the same back and smiles but it stops before it reaches his eyes. He continues to busy himself with tidying, not looking back at me. He probably thinks I'm a right nosey freak.

My doorbell rings so I get up to answer it, taking my wine with me. I must get onto the property management company and get them to fix the main doors, now I'm a woman living on my own I don't feel too safe knowing that just anyone can come up and be right outside my door. They'll probably still use the virus as an excuse not to fix it yet. At least I have my spyhole now, I peer through and smile at Beau and Laura's grinning faces.

'Hi guys, come on in.' I open the door, sounding cheerier than I feel after seeing Flynn's unamused face across the balconies.

'Wow, Alannah, you look stunning,' Laura says.

'Thanks, Laura, you're looking gorgeous too,' I reply as she beams at me. She's wearing one of my creations. A 1950's style tea-dress in an animal print fabric consisting of giraffes, elephants and monkeys. Sadly, for her, I couldn't get any newt fabric.

'Let us in then, sis,' Beau chirps, jangling his bag of booze.

'Sorry, yes come in, come in.' I step back and motion for them to come to the kitchen, wobbling in my heels. I'm already unsteady on my feet after not wearing them for months. My feet certainly aren't used to this, they've morphed into flat hobbit feet which are really hard to stuff into heels now.

'Want one? I've got elderflower gin and tonic,' Laura sings.

'Sounds perfect, yes please.' I grab some glasses and place them on the worktop.

Laura pours us all a drink while I fetch the ice out of the freezer.

'Let's go and sit outside ladies, it's stuffy as hell in here,' Beau suggests as I plonk a few lumps of ice into our glasses.

'Really? No, let's sit indoors. I was out there earlier and it's way hotter out there than it is in here,' I try feebly.

'You're insane.' Beau wipes his forehead then waltzes outside onto the balcony anyway, in typical Beau form. Laura shrugs at me as if to say he's right then follows him out.

We spend the next hour chatting and laughing as I steal glances over at Flynn's flat. Beau and Laura tell me that they have booked to go on a ten-day silent retreat in Valencia, just before Christmas. I spit my drink out, the thought of either of them not talking for ten hours let alone ten days makes me howl. Beau will almost definitely implode. They want to connect with themselves and each other on a deeper level. To be fair they both laughed too so I'm not sure how serious they're taking it, it will certainly be an experience for them. I can't wait to hear the stories when they come back and hopefully by then they won't need to quarantine when they come back.

The gin is definitely helping me to relax. Flynn's sitting down on his sofa now, looking at his phone. I wonder if he's going out too? I could potentially bump into him so I'm glad I'm looking my best. We finish our third round of drinks and my stomach rumbles loudly. I'm feeling rather lightheaded and my body needs food. We trot down the stairs to wait for our taxi. The shoes are really hurting my feet now. I did consider changing them on the way out but I don't really have anything else that goes with this dress so vanity won out and I'll just have to suffer. I'm about five steps away from the taxi when I glance up at Flynn's flat. He's sitting at his dining room table with his much-awaited dinner guest.

Becky.

I gasp then try to focus on my walking, which is becoming quite difficult.

'Wait guys, I can't walk in these shoes very well,' I moan, stumbling after them, feeling like one of the giraffes on Laura's dress.

'Ouuuchhhhhh,' I scream at the top of my lungs, hardly recognising the animalistic nose that I'm making as the heel of my shoe gets caught in the pavement and I go flying. Both knees are bleeding like I'm a four-year-old who's fallen hard off her bike for the first time. I've fallen arse over tit on the hard floor and it hurts. It really hurts. Laura runs to my rescue as Beau halts the taxi.

'Oh, mate, are you okay?' Laura helps me up, giggling quietly.

'If it wasn't so painful, I'd be laughing too. My knees,' I complain.

'I'm so sorry for laughing. Oh, Alannah, your shoe. The heel's come off.' Laura lifts it up and waves the floppy heel in front of my face.

'Oh noooo,' I wail, looking helplessly at my broken shoe then again at my dress which has my blood all over it. At that moment I make the mistake of glancing up and see Flynn and Becky on his balcony. Flynn stares at me horrified whilst Becky's big gob is wide open, her mocking laughter cackling and echoing all around me.

What the hell is she doing at his flat?

The dogging bitch.

Chapter Twenty

A week later . . .September 14th 2020

This morning, I woke up to the news that Boris has hit us with the rule of six again.

We're only allowed to see six people inside or outside our homes at once. It doesn't really affect me as I don't see that many people at once anyway but for some reason it's got me feeling a little low. I know it's necessary to curb the virus as cases have increased again but I can't help but feel restrained and afraid, trapped in a draconian society. Before all of this, we were so free and we really had no idea. My hands are red raw from all the washing and sanitising that I have to do as I'm handling material that the girls are working with. No amount of moisturiser is helping these dry, scaly, tired hands.

I've just about recovered from what was meant to be a fun night of frolics. My knees have scabbed over and now they just look like eleven-year-old boy knees as opposed to four-year-old girl knees. At least they don't hurt anymore. We didn't make it to the taxi that night. Beau sent the driver away with some money for his trouble. Laura bundled me up and helped me hobble up the stairs, broken shoe in hand. We stayed inside the flat, drinking the rest of the gin. A greasy take away was ordered and we giggled and surmised about what Becky was doing in Flynn's flat. Beau went out onto the balcony a few times to 'get some air' and came back after about the third time reporting that Becky seemed to have gone as the curtains had closed, either that or they wanted some privacy. My heart sinks at the thought of them rekindling their relationship. I just don't get it. Flynn was adamant he was over her and he was disgusted at what she'd done with dog boy. I just can't see him forgiving her that easily but why was she there if not for reconciliation?

I make my way over to Beau's flat for a coffee break and some lunch, for some reason I haven't been inside his flat since lockdown, he's always just come to mine. It will be nice to have a change of scenery and to drink lots of much-needed coffee.

'Yo, Sis,' Beau greets me as he opens the door. 'Come in, come in.'

'Wow, flat's looking nice, I like it,' I comment as I take in the clean, fresh and tidy apartment. He's painted the living room walls navy blue and above the sofa hangs one of Laura's paintings of a beach. I know it's Laura's because she has the same one in her house. On the opposite wall is a painting of a sunset, it's stunning. I stand there staring at it for a second, wishing I could dive in and get lost in it. Beau's saxophone sits proudly adjacent to his TV. Next to his sofa is a huge purple crystal that stands about two foot tall. It's beautiful and I want one.

'Amethyst,' he states as he catches me eyeing it up. 'It's a great stone to have in your living room, great for anything really. It has real healing energy.

'It's very grand, must have cost a bomb.'

'It did but I can afford it now Laura lives here,' Beau announces, puffing out his chest.

'What? She's moved in already? Go you, Casanova!' I punch him playfully on the arm. I'm a bit put out she didn't tell me. Am I that much of a miserable wench that they are treading on eggshells around me now? I feel guilty that they feel that way and make a mental note to message Laura later. I've been pushing all of my friends away and I didn't have that many to begin with, come to think of it I haven't heard from Lisa in months either.

'Yep, I've finally grown up and got me a girlfriend and she's a good one too,' Beau boasts.

'She sure is, don't mess it up. Where is she anyway?' My eyes dart around his flat, expecting her to jump out at any minute.

'No chance of that, Sis. Oh, she's at work.' Beau pads over to the kitchen to turn the kettle on and I plonk myself down on his sofa. I notice a load of paper work sitting on the side.

'What's all this stuff?' I call out to him, picking up the huge wedge of paper.

'What stuff?'

'Paper work for something.'

'I'm learning reiki, hence all the stones. My aim is to become a reiki master and give up my shitty day job. I've been doing it all online but the course leader sent us some stuff in the post. He's a bit old school, I told him he shouldn't be wasting the paper if he cares about the planet.' Beau brings in our drinks.

'Course you did, Greta Thunberg.' I laugh. 'Beats working in a factory I guess.'

'Yeah, I think it's my calling.' Beau sits down beside

me as he frowns and nods to himself. He sets down the cups of coffee and a pack of ginger biscuits on a small table that looks like a polished tree stump.

'So, I spoke to Flynn about Becky,' Beau blurts out and I choke on the biscuit I was so very much enjoying. Crumbs fly out and Beau makes a face like I'm the most gross person ever as he wipes bits of wet ginger biscuit off his face.

'Revolting, Sis, you don't want to be doing that in public.'

'Well, I doubt anyone is going to tell me unnerving news like this in public. What did you say to him?'

'Just asked him, what was Becky big bum doing at his flat.'

'You didn't call her that . . .'

'Well yeah, and I told him that's what you call her too.' Beau smirks and crosses his gangly legs, looking pleased with himself.

'You . . .' I make a fist to punch him again with every intention of giving him a dead arm this time.

'Chill, chill out, man, course I didn't,' Beau protests as he dodges my attempt at punching him. 'He said that Becky came over because she wanted to apologise and get closure. He's not taking her back and has no interest in her whatsoever. They had a few house things to sort out and he took it as an opportunity to be civil. I guess he wants to keep her onside so she doesn't carry on bad mouthing him,' he continues. 'Oh, and he asked about you.' Beau raises both eyebrows and points at me.

'About me?' I point to myself.

'Yeah, he asked how you were after your fall.' Beau dives onto the floor, screaming help me help me in a high feminine voice. I stare at him, not impressed at his impersonation of me.

'Get up. My fall? You make me sound about eighty. I didn't have a fall, I tripped over in the stupid heels that I should never have worn.' A pang of sadness hits me. Bet had an actual fall, poor Bet. I so miss our chats. Every time I go out onto the balcony, I keep expecting to see her little cheery face pop up behind her beautiful hanging baskets. The new neighbour seems nice enough, a girl around my age, but it will take some getting used to.

'But he isn't taking her back, that's good,' Beau offers as he sits back on the sofa after his performance.

'Yeah, that is good, my gut sank for a second when I saw them,' I admit.

'I know, Sis, your face said it all.'

'Did it?'

'Yep, you're so transparent but that's a good thing in a way, you wear your heart on your sleeve. Lots of people struggle with emotions these days, not helped by social media and hiding behind a keyboard. No one talks in person anymore.'

'Okay, Doctor Phil, don't give up your day job just yet.'

Beau guffaws and I snort laugh along with him.

'Seriously though, I think I'm falling for Flynn. I can't stop thinking about him.' There we go, I've said it out loud.

'I know.'

'Could you sense it through your crystals?' I snigger.

'Yeah, something like that, you're my Sis, don't forget, I know you better than anyone.'

'Yeah, you're probably right.'

'So, what's next?' Beau asks, uncrossing his gangly legs and folding his arms behind his head.

'What do you mean?'

'What are you going to do about it?' he asks, like there's no other option than to do something about it.

'There's not a lot I can do about it, is there? He isn't replying to any of my messages since he saw me with Daniel.'

'Come on. You have to grab life by the balls like you have with your dressmaking. Now it's time to sort the love life out.' Beau reaches one gangly arm out and air grabs the imaginary balls. I imagine Flynn's homemade shit balls and it makes me smile. 'Seriously man, Flynn's a wounded pigeon, you've got to remember he's been wronged by Becky so his trust is broken. If he isn't replying to you then it's because you have to prove that you aren't like her. You've got to do something big.'

I'm not sure about Flynn being a wounded pigeon he's more of an elegant gazelle but I guess Beau's right about grabbing life by the balls. I think I distanced myself from Jake when he started acting strangely at the start of lockdown, my gut knew something wasn't right. I literally have no feelings towards him whatsoever now. I'm numb to him. I thought I'd be wallowing in misery for years, unable to feel anything for anyone else for a very long time, but it seems not. Once I got over the initial hurt and shock, it's become easier and easier. I've surprised myself, and I'm pretty proud of myself. Of course, it also helps that I haven't seen or heard from him since he moved out. Out of sight, out of mind and all that.

'Okay, Doctor Love Crystal, what do you suggest?'

'Well, I had this idea…

Beau proceeds to tell me in great detail how I can win Flynn over. He explains it has to be some sort of grand gesture as Flynn's clearly a little hurt. His idea isn't too cringeworthy but it's certainly out of my comfort zone. I laugh and tell him to bugger off at first, it's too brave, too bold and possibly could be seen as a little desperate if I don't do it right. But Beau is correct, if I don't do it, I'll never know. Someone like Flynn will get snapped up by another Beckyesq big bum in no time. So, it's now or never.

I guess, I've just got to grab life by the shit balls.

♥ ♥ ♥

'Oh, hi ummmm, I live up there in one of the flats. I think my friend's drone flew into your garden by accident. Could I have it back please?' I babble awkwardly as Baldy Man answers the door and stares at me with a poker face from underneath his full-face visor. His face looks very serious but his clothes don't. He's wearing very bright orange shorts and a white wife-beater vest with the slogan 'Be Happy' written on it in neon pink.

'Oh, of course my love, I was wondering where that came from.' He chuckles in an unusually high voice and his face lights up. He looks kind when he smiles. He's one of those people where the voice doesn't match the face. I expected it to be all deep and husky, like Phil Mitchel from EastEnders but he sounds more like Alan Carr.

'Thanks so much,' I reply.

He nods and goes back inside to fetch it. Moments later Baldy Man arrives with Flynn's drone and the remote. A very battered drone. Along with his face visor, he is now also donning yellow rubber gloves while he carries the drone on what looks like a pizza paddle with a very long handle.

'Here you go, my love. It's a bit broken, isn't it?

Might have to get a new one. Oddly, the remote came down with it.' He frowns before holding out the pizza paddle and I step back to take the drone, being careful to not touch the paddle as I'm not wearing gloves, or a mask for that matter. I feel a little underdressed. He pulls a face that looks a bit guilty but I know it's not his fault. I saw it crash.

'Yeah, looks like it,' I agree. 'But thanks anyway, he might be able to fix it.' I smile. 'My friend will appreciate having it back,' I add.

'No problem, tell your friend thanks for the toilet roll.' He chuckles again and I chuckle nervously along with him as I watch his visor steam up with his breath. 'I could have done with that at the beginning of lockdown when we couldn't get any, I had to be creative and come up with my own ways of keeping clean,' he continues and the mental video of him giving himself a colonic with his hose plays in my mind. 'Absolute nightmare it was, my love. We were halfway through getting the bathroom re-fitted when all this happened so we were having to improvise. Absolute hell I tell you, the house was a building site for months after the fitters abandoned it, we've only recently got it finished.' His voice is even higher-pitched now, and he's shaking his head vigorously with one hand on his hip. The visor wobbles along with him and I wonder if he wears that all the time or just to answer the door.

'I can imagine.' The image of his hose and naked bum burns into my retinas once more. I can NEVER unsee that.

'Anyway.' He shakes his wobbly visor head again. 'I'm Vic by the way, nice to meet you.'

'I'm Alannah, nice to meet you too.'

♥ ♥ ♥

I look at the little drone staring back at me. I'm questioning whether it's man enough to make it to the other side, even after Beau's expert fixing job. But there's no use in worrying about that now, I have to try. I spend the next few days practicing, flying it around the flat and I've crashed it quite a few times, it doesn't seem to go where I want it to go. I'm lucky I haven't broken it. Yet. Beau even comes over to give me a lesson. It's no good, it appears I'm very shit at flying drones, it's certainly not one of my talents. Beau suggested flying it over for me but I told him no, it's *my* romantic gesture. Not his.

We've had a few practises this morning though and I've finally twigged how to fly it and get it to go where I want it to. I'm feeling pretty chuffed with myself. I fold up my note and attach it to the drone, sticking it on with double-sided tape, I hope it stays on and it doesn't fall off for some stranger to pick up and see. Oh, how embarrassing, nothing happens in Coolsbay so something like that would be sure to make the local newspaper. I can see the headline now. *Mysterious love note found on beach promenade – Coolsbay appeal to find owner.*

'Why am I doing this?' I ask, suddenly aware that this idea is ridiculous. 'Surely sending Flynn a message from my phone would be a lot more socially acceptable, normal and a lot less bunny boiler.' I examine the drone in my hand and wonder if I could just throw it over. No, perhaps not, it wouldn't have the same affect.

'No, believe me, he will love it. Blokes don't usually receive romantic gestures from birds but the truth is we do want them and why shouldn't we get them. We need TLC too.' Beau shrugs his shoulders.

I'm not so convinced now. 'Really?' I say.

'Yes, really.' Beau nods and frowns. All serious.

'Okay, maybe you're right, if it works that is… Oh, and Beau…'

'Yeah?'

'Don't call women birds, okay.'

'Chill, Sis, chill.'

Chapter Twenty-One

I've sent Beau away so I can do this on my own. Today is the day.

Laura should be home from work around now so I sent a quick message suggesting she take him away from the flat for dinner or something. As much as I adore my brother, the last thing I want is an audience of Beau hanging over the balcony cheering me on. It will be potentially cringe-worthy enough, without him doing that. I've taken the note off the drone and re-written it four times now but I think I'm happy with the final draft. It's to the point, clear and not too desperate.

I hope.

Beau's advice was to be clear as most men don't generally get hints and I tend to agree with him based on my experience with Jake, so that's what I've done in my note to Flynn. I creep out onto the balcony because I don't want Flynn to see me at first. It would be ideal for him to come out on to the balcony once it's landed or even after but I really don't want him watching me fly it, too much pressure and his look of befuddlement may inadvertently put me off. He should be coming out onto his balcony soon, he normally comes out at dusk to get his washing in on a Tuesday, a creature of habit.

My hands are shaking as I set the remote down on the outdoor table. Next, I set the drone down on a stack of books that I've piled on top of the table so that it sits above the level of the balcony rails.

I watched loads of videos on YouTube of people holding the drone out with one hand and it taking off from there but I don't trust my trembling palms right now and I've been using flat surfaces to practice taking off indoors so that will have to do.

With one shaking hand I pick up the remote control and adjust the drone with the other so that it's facing towards Flynn's balcony. I just have to get on with it. The rose quartz stone is sitting next to the stack of books and I pick it up after adjusting the drone, just rolling it in between my thumb and finger. Feeling its smoothness and imagining its good, positive love vibrations. I've become a little obsessed with these stones, whether they work or not, they give me something else to focus on, to help calm my nerves and 'recentre', as Beau would put it.

Come on, Alannah.

Deep breaths.

My thumb flicks the switch of the controller and the drone takes off from the stack of books, as I hold my breath. We're off to a good start. I must say it's taken off beautifully, gliding over my balcony rails and heading towards Flynn's flat. Wow, it's really picking up some speed, I don't remember it going this fast in the living room but I guess the distance is much further out here and it has more time to pick up some speed.

Flynn steps out onto the balcony right on cue to get his washing in and I almost lose my focus. In my peripheral vision he smiles quizzically at me and it spurs me on to keep concentrating and get the drone to him safely. He spots it, smiles and holds out his arms and hands, and it looks like it might just land neatly in his palms. Oh, how perfect would that be? Wow. I *am* a pro at this. I slowly exhale. I am an expert drone flyer. No sooner are these thoughts out there than the drone picks up more momentum, I mean really picks up momentum and takes on a life of its own. Just like I did with Flynn.

This shitty drone is cursed.

I should have known better and got a new one. The angry little thing aggressively flies towards poor Flynn's forehead. There's nothing I can do. I'm desperately flicking every switch and the drone is doing nothing but heading straight for him. Flynn's expression changes and he goes about ducking this way and that, hiding behind his washing, trying to avoid the drone as it flies around after him. I go to shout but nothing comes out. I've turned the drone off but somehow it still has power in it. Driving itself forward and aiming for its target, Flynn tries desperately to dodge it again but makes a massive error in judgement. He goes the wrong way, taking a huge lunge sideways and forwards, appearing from behind two pairs of boxer shorts hanging on his washing line, straight into the path of the drone. It's too late. The drone smacks Flynn perfectly right between the eyes with a big thwack.

'Ouch,' Flynn howls, his hand flying up to the space between his eyebrows. Poor guy. I bet the last thing he was expecting when he woke up this morning was to be attacked by his own angry, flying drone.

'I'm so sorry,' I call out to him, cringing. 'Are you okay?' I wait a few seconds. He doesn't reply. He's on the floor still rubbing his brow, frowning. It's then I realise that he's peeling off the note, unfolding it and is about to read it. I hold my breath and clench my eyes shut, rooted to the spot with fear and anticipation.

Dear Flynn,

If you're reading this letter, it's made its way over to you by power of your almighty drone. I hope this isn't too weird but I feel like I should explain a few things to you and writing them down just comes easier.

1. *I rescued your drone from the baldy guy in the maisonette and found out why he was using a hose to wash his bum – their builder abandoned their bathroom refurb at the beginning of lockdown. The drone was sadly broken, but me and Beau have fixed it. I hope.*
2. *I got a little jealous when I saw Becky at your flat recently, Beau told me you weren't getting back together. I can't lie, that made me rather happy.*
3. *The guy you saw at my house with the flowers, his name is Daniel, he's just an old friend from work who may have wanted more but I can promise you, I didn't. Although I can appreciate how the flowers may have made it look.*
4. *I'm over Jake – totally.*
5. *I miss you – so much.*
6. *I hope all of the above points are clear on how I truly feel about you.*
7. *The ball/drone is in your court/balcony.*

Alannah xx

I breath in the Indian summer air through my nose and slowly open one eye at a time as I breath out. My eyes are instantly drawn to the sky above Flynn's flat which has transformed into a backdrop of oranges, pinks and purples. I gasp because it's so stunning. I don't think I've ever seen the sky look so vibrant, so rich and so full of life. So full of something familiar, something I've needed a lot of these past few months, something to keep us all going when there's not been much else.

Hope.

As the day fades into night Flynn's body morphs rapidly into a silhouette, I can just about make out that he's facing in my direction. He could be watching me but it's too dark to see his expression, I can't gauge whether he's happy, amused, uncomfortable, disgusted or pissed off. He screws up something in his hand. My note. Gets up and marches back into his flat, not looking back. No attempt to speak to me, no sign of how he feels.

Gutted. I'm just gutted.

It starts to rain. Drizzling at first and then the big drops fall hard and fast, soaking me wet through as I stand there in a daze of regret, humiliation and stupidity. I should never have listened to Beau. The rain washes away the bright colours of the sunset and the sky turns black, an ominous representation of my fate. I'm going to need to move house now, I think dramatically. How can I ever face him again? Maybe I can move to Mooloolaba, as far away as possible. I slowly pick up the books and the remote control and slope back inside my flat.

My phone's buzzing on the sofa, I glance over and see it's Beau, dying to know how it went, I expect. I can't answer that just yet. The intercom buzzes and I groan, evidently Beau will not wait. After months of it being broken, the property management company finally fixed the front door, which is a good thing, at least there's less chance of me being murdered in my own flat now. Beau is so impatient. I press on the buzzer and speak into it with a hoarse voice.

'No, it definitely did not go to plan. Come up for all the cringeworthy details. By the way I don't believe in those stupid magic stones and I don't believe in love anymore,' I huff at him then hang up, not giving Beau a chance to reply.

There's now a dark mass building up in my chest and I need to let it out. Scream. Cry. Be sick. Something. Moments later there's a knock at my door. I pad over and open it without looking through the spyhole.

I know who it is.

But it's not.

'It's you,' I mumble, untucking my hair from behind my ears to hide my blushing, hot cheeks. My chest feels like it's going to explode, the mass is melting fast and it's travelling through my veins with the rapidity of a bush fire.

'Yeah. It's me,' Flynn says softly. He's soaking wet too, looking more gorgeous than ever and all I want to do is pin him down and kiss him. Is that even allowed? I'm not even sure of all the rules anymore.

'Sorry, I thought you were… I mean… it's Beau he…'

Flynn shakes his head and runs his fingers through his wet hair before rubbing his arms to warm himself. He steps closer, but not close enough.

'Don't worry, but I want to know more about these magic stones. Sounds intriguing.' He laughs, eyes shining with happiness. Then he's looking at me, I mean *really* looking at me. Drinking me in. And it's all the more intense because he's far enough away that he can see all of me.

I bite my bottom lip and look down, suddenly self-conscious of the fact I'm wet through too. His gaze is still on me; my face and neck tingle as I look back up at him. He frowns, faintly at first as if trying to figure out what to say, there's probably a lot to talk about. Then he smiles slowly before speaking.

'I miss you too. I've always missed not being with you.'

'Really?' I grin back at him. Surprised, relieved, elated.

'Really.' He nods.

Flynn stands there as we stare at each other intensely. Both grinning from ear to ear, both soaking wet. A couple of drowned, but happy, rats.

I wonder what he's thinking, but I can't imagine it's far off what I'm thinking. I imagine him gently taking my face in both his hands, they'll still be slightly cold from being outside in the rain but that will just feel nice on my hot, flustered face. I'm staring at him, willing him to make the move. It's okay.

Before I know what's happening Flynn grabs my waist, pulling me close to him and my hands fly up to his face like a magnet. His stubble is rough but his lips feel like the softest of velvet when he kisses me, tenderly at first, then more firmly, more eager. His hands caress the back of my neck and hair while shivers run down my spine as we become entwined in our own intense beautiful bubble. In a completely unperfect and uncertain world, more so than ever before in my lifetime, this moment is entirely perfect and it was definitely worth the wait.

Chapter Twenty-two

'Alannah, have you got any Buck's Fizz? Let's get this party started.' Beau slings one long arm around Laura, knocking a couple of silver baubles off my Christmas tree in the process. He makes no attempt to pick them up before eyeing up my bottle of champagne sitting on the drinks cabinet. He reaches over and grabs it, nodding his head in approval with a glint in his eye.

'Buck's Fizz? Don't you dare ruin my champagne, Beau, no orange juice is going in these bubbles.' I flash Laura a knowing smile whilst snatching away the champagne and plonk down a bottle of cava and orange juice in its place. Beau raises both eyebrows then shrugs his shoulders before picking up the cava to open it. No, this champagne will be saved just for us later I think, just for Flynn and I when we celebrate.

He'll be here any minute.

The door buzzes and my stomach heats up with excitement, today is going to be perfect, it already is.

'Hello gorgeous boy, I've missed you,' I smoulder into the intercom with a big grin on my face.

'It's Mum, darling. I'm not a boy or at least I wasn't the last time I checked.' Mum giggles hysterically, sounds like she's already had a Buck's Fizz or two.

'*I'm* a boy,' Mum's partner Gary pipes up in the background.

'No, you're an old man, my dear.' Mum laughs and Gary playfully says, 'Oi.'

'Oh, Mum, Gary, so sorry, come up.' I blush and quickly buzz them in.

'Happy Christmas, sweetheart,' Mum sings as I open the door to them, all happy, yet flustered. Gary's standing beside her laden with bags of presents, grinning but sounding very out of puff from the stairs.

'Happy Christmas.' I give her and Gary a big warm hug before ushering them into my flat to see the others.

'Buck's Fizz, guys?' Beau asks as we enter the room, whilst pouring himself a sizeable glass, he goes to pour Laura one before she places a hand over the glass, stopping him.

'Just orange juice for me remember.' Laura smiles sweetly at Beau, placing one hand on her stomach. Beau nods and places his hand on top of hers as they grin at each other, lost in their own little world.

'Oh, yes please, happy Christmas you two.' Mum grins and claps her hands together, then strides over to them as Gary dumps the presents by the Christmas tree. She wraps both Laura and Beau up in her arms, giving them a big long bear hug. Gary sidles over to shake Beau's hand and gives Laura an awkward pat on the side of her arm whilst Mum carries on smothering them. Gary's very sweet, but I guess he feels a bit out of it as we haven't really seen him for months. He's a quiet guy anyway but the virus made him a bit of a hermit, more so than required. Mum finally untangles herself from them both and stands back to appraise Laura.

'Oh, Laura, you look absolutely glowing, how many weeks now?' Mum gently places her hand on Laura's stomach and Laura smiles, patting her hand to let her know it's okay.

'Fifteen weeks now,' Laura announces proudly, I'm feeling so much better. I think that's why we had such a hard time at the retreat. I was just so sick and I had to suffer in silence, literally. I thought I'd be over the worse by the time we went away but it lasted a little longer than expected.' Laura grimaces and glances at Beau who mirrors her cringing expression. They're so cute.

'Oh sweetheart,' I don't know why you two ever wanted to do that nonsense anyway, it baffled me. Beau not talking for ten days, it's almost impossible.'

'It was impossible, wasn't it?' I tease and Laura giggles. She can laugh now but they weren't laughing at the time. A ten-day silent retreat in Valencia resulted in Laura puking pretty much the whole time and Beau being overly protective, glaring at everyone and eventually shouting at someone. No, it didn't quite go to plan.

'We did it but it was so hard,' Beau explains, then takes a big gulp of his Buck's Fizz. 'Being silent does mad shit to you, man. You live with people for ten days that you've spoken to for all of one hour at the beginning of the retreat, wash each others' dishes, build fires and cook dinner together. You feel like a family, man, but you also get irrational thoughts. Even though you don't know these people, you build up all these ideas of what they're like and they aren't always good.'

'Yes, or true, like that poor man you thought wanted to steal me away, even when I accidently puked all over myself and on his feet.' Laura purses her lips at Beau and rubs her stomach.

'Yeah, he did, he kept glaring at you, like, *I want that*

woman. So, I had to assert myself and let him know that you were with me. Plus, he was way too touchy-feely, cleaning up all your vomit.' Beau shudders.

'It was on his feet, he had to clean it up. Rather him than you though,' Laura adds, chuckling.

'Hmm, it all sounds very caveman-like,' Mum muses as Beau proceeds to act like he's a chimp picking fleas out of Laura's hair and eating them. This kid's going to have one embarrassing dad, but also an extremely fun one.

'Mum, you have no idea,' Beau warns, suddenly turning serious. 'You connect with everyone on a much deeper level, that's why I've given up social media. It's evil, man and so superficial.'

'I'll have to agree with you there, my boy. He does have his head screwed on, doesn't he, Alannah?' Mum asks, looking all proud of golden boy as he puffs out his pigeon chest. The reiki master, love guru. He drives me insane but I love him dearly. I couldn't ask for a better brother.

'Yes, Mum, he does now.' I smirk and Beau gives me one of his silent retreat glares. What Mum doesn't know is that Beau used to smoke between eight to ten joints a day and he certainly didn't have his head screwed on then. Not being able to get any weed during lockdown has done him the world of good. I know Laura wouldn't have gone near him if he'd still been a stoner and now, they're having a baby. Mum will finally have her first grandchild and she's over the moon. Watching my family here on Christmas day, including Laura who's also my best friend, makes me feel all warm, happy and fuzzy inside, there's just one person missing.

Where is he?

Just as the thought enters my head, the intercom buzzes again and I leap up to answer it, leaving everyone chatting and laughing in the living room.

'Hey you, I've missed you,' I murmur into the speaker.

'I've missed you too, even though it's only been a few hours,' Flynn murmurs back and I can hear the smile in his voice.

'Come up.' I buzz him in but as I do something white catches my eye on the floor. I kick the doormat up and look down to see a white envelope which is partially hidden by the doormat. I bend down and pick it up, it's a letter, although it looks like it could be a Christmas card, though you don't get many of those nowadays. I pick the envelope up and turn it over, examining it, before feeling a pain in the pit of my stomach. I recognise the handwriting on the envelope.

Jake's.

Flynn's already knocking at the door so I open it with the letter in my hand. He looks lovely in a burgundy scarf, jeans and a loud Christmas jumper, but I can't focus.

'What's up, you look like you've seen the holy ghost.' Flynn looks at me quizzically before kissing me on the cheek, he follows my gaze down to the letter clasped in my hand and frowns.

'I think it's from Jake,' I exclaim wide-eyed.

'Oh. Open it?'

I let out a small sigh and slowly start to open the letter. May as well get it out of the way, he's probably demanding more stuff from the flat. What a time to do it, at Christmas. I stare up at Flynn, hesitating at opening it in front of him.

'I'll leave you to it, gorgeous. Let me know what it

says later, but only if you want to.' Flynn touches my arm then kisses me again, leaving a burning imprint on my cheek before striding off into the living room to say hello to everyone. I smile a small smile to myself as I hear a big roar of laughter at what sounds like Beau taking the piss out of Flynn's festive jumper.

Let's get this out of the way.

I take a deep breath and, like a plaster, I rip the rest of it open.

Dear Alannah,

I found your letter in the box when I was unpacking recently, so I wanted to reply to you and set the record straight. You deserve it. Now I'm away from you I can see I may have been a bit of a dick. At the time I didn't realise how much of a dick I was babe, I'm sorry about that.

I don't want you back, this isn't a begging letter but I guess you kind of deserve to know the truth about what happened with me and Cheska. We are together now and we are bringing up our little boy, I'm catching up on all the years I missed and am really enjoying being a dad. I'm sorry you had to get caught up in it all. So sorry.

Me and Cheska met twelve years ago at work and as gooey as it sounds, it was love at first sight for both of us but it was very complicated. Cheska had a boyfriend and I was very young, she left the job at the gym and I didn't see her for years, although we always kept in touch apart from about a year before I met you (she had a new boyfriend). The day after you and I met, Cheska got back in touch, you have to understand I didn't know where it was going to go with you then. I was so young, just a lad and not really ready to settle down.

Anyway to cut a long story short, we started meeting up, then Cheska found out I was seeing someone else (you) and she left, she was pregnant at the time but didn't know. When she found out she thought about telling me but at that point she said she was so hurt she just couldn't tell me and wanted it just to be her and the baby. Then she met someone else, he then left her for someone else, much younger too. It's all a mess I know but it's made us realise our love for each other and our family. We were meant to be together.

I hope this explains things a bit babe. I hear you're with Flynn now anyway, I'm not surprised.

Good luck with that, he broke my nose.

Jake
xx

A single tear runs down my cheek as my shoulders bob up and down uncontrollably. I swiftly wipe the tear away. But I'm not crying, I'm laughing, hysterically. This letter is an absolute joke and if I'm honest, I'm embarrassed to show it to anyone. I'm actually quite disgusted with myself for ever being with such an idiot. It does make me wonder if Cheska knew who I was all along though, was the eggs incident pre-meditated? I'll never know and I'm just fine with that now. She obviously hasn't vetted this letter as he still refers to me as 'babe'.

He's paid me back now so I don't have to deal with him ever again, or at least his Mum paid me. I screw the letter up in my hand and stuff it in my pocket. This is going straight in the bin, where it belongs. And no, I don't regret being with you, Jake, we were together way too long, but I've learnt a lot from you and you led me to Flynn who is just perfect.

I walk into the living room and it's all eyes on me for a second before Gary manages to choke on some Buck's Fizz and Mum jumps up to the rescue. Amongst the kerfuffle, I lock eyes with Flynn and head over to him.

'Everything alright?' Flynn asks with a look of concern in his eyes.

'Yep, all fine.' I flash him a bright smile and sit down beside him, taking his hand in mine.

'So, shall we tell them the news? I whisper to Flynn as everyone gets over Gary's choking trauma and back to festive bickering and bantering.

'Yes, let's do it, which bit first?' he whispers back. I give him a gentle kiss on the lips then lightly tap my finger on his chest. Flynn clears his throat and uses a spoon to ding on his glass and get everyone's attention.

'Speech! Speech!' Beau's big voice booms around the room as he catches wind of Flynn's unnoticed glass dinging.

'Thanks, Beau. Alannah and I have an announcement to make. Well actually two announcements, I guess,' Flynn declares to the room before he hesitates and looks to me. 'Yep so, drum roll please.'

In true Beau form, he proceeds to bang on the table as I watch my poor wine glasses jump up and down, Bucks Fizz sloshing all over my coffee table.

'Flynn and I are moving in together!' I interject to stop Beau banging the shit out of my coffee table even more. He stops then grabs my champagne and strides over to pour Flynn and I a glass. 'Well, he's moving in here,' I continue, wincing as Beau pops the champagne bottle inches from my face. I suggested it this morning and he said yes. We want to be close; we want to wake up with each other every day. And why not?

'Oh, sweetheart that's great news, not a bit soon though?' Mum asks, concerned that we haven't been dating for a year before moving in together.

'It's fine mum, it's what we want.'

'Okay, well as long as you're happy.' Mum glides over to give us both a kiss on the cheek as the others whoop and cheer, chinking glasses with Flynn and I.

'And the other news,' I add, after Mum has sat down again.

'Not preggers are you? Don't steal our sunshine!' Beau jokes, raising an eyebrow.

'Oh my God, that would be amazing, pregnant together!' Laura gasps then starts to tear up as Beau rubs her back, grinning at her.

'No, no, no. Don't jump the gun, guys.' I blush. With Jake that's all I ever wanted but at the moment I'm too selfish to share Flynn with anyone else. I just want him all to myself for a little while.

'Flynn's bought us tickets to fly out to Mooloolaba to visit Bet's son, Richard who owns a clothes boutique,' I squeak, squeezing his hand with excitement.

'He bought me the tickets when I told him that Richard had expressed an interest in my dresses and wants to invest in my business here in the UK. So, Flynn said the polite thing to do is to go and have a business meeting with him, in Australia. He arranged it all with Richard without me even knowing, we're going to stay with them for a few days and then travel around Australia, for three weeks.'

'Oh wow, how lucky are you!' Mum says as Gary nods along. She's twinkly eyed as she grins at Flynn, I think she's sold on him moving in now. He's clearly going to look after her daughter.

'She deserves it, well done, Flynn, it's so exciting. Your dresses and mask combinations have gone viral now. No wonder Bet's son has an interest in the business,' Laura pipes up and I catch Beau, the anti-social media activist rolling his eyes at the word viral.

'Yeah, remember us when you hit the big-time, Sis.' Beau rubs his fingers together to infer I'll be making a lot of money. I hope so.

'It's very exciting, I'm so grateful. I can't wait to get started and work with Bet's son. I'm going to have my very own shop. I can't quite believe it. Who would have thought all this would happen in lockdown? New career, new man, new life.' I grin like a Cheshire cat at Flynn then take a sip of my champagne as I watch everyone cheering and buzzing for our new adventures. Next door's wreath on their balcony catches my eye and I take a moment to remember Bet who would normally have a Christmas flower arrangement out there. She helped make a lot of this possible. When times were feeling particularly tough, I remember her saying to me, *'Difficult roads often lead to beautiful destinations, Alannah.'* And in this case, she was so right.

The End.

Other books by Belle Henderson

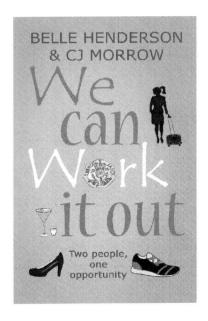

Printed in Great Britain
by Amazon